Praise for *Anchored*

"Katy Goforth's voice in *Anchored* is so authentic and sensual, and her characters so well told you can smell them, that her stories will take you back to a memory you never had. But you'd swear you lived it. In other words, *Anchored* does exactly what good storytelling should do. Goforth's collection is an achievement."

—**Adam Van Winkle**, author of *Dylan Quick Is a Dairy Queen Don Quixote* and Editor-in-Chief of Cowboy Jamboree Press

"Katy Goforth's debut hybrid collection is anchored by memorable touchpoints: pop culture, rural America, family, friends, growing up, fitting in, ghosts, and grief. From harvest-gold carpet and Corelle Butterfly Gold dishes to Sweet Valley High Books and Dr Pepper Lip Smackers, the stories are identifiable, spunky, and vulnerable. Whether her characters are drinking from Styrofoam political cups or eating potluck meals together, Goforth's endearing voice invites us to be her neighbor too. Her collection anchors readers with narratives that blur truth and fiction, dressed up with some Cherries in the Snow lipstick."

—**Amy Cipolla Barnes**, author of *Child Craft* and *Ambrotypes*

"A tender daydream blurring the lines between fact and fiction, *Anchored* reaches beneath a surface coated with who we are: all the diesel fumes, White Shoulders perfume, *The Young and the Restless* theme song, red lipstick, lemon pound cake, and tiny bottles of Fireball to capture who we yearn to be, and to find the true core of the South: family, both blood and found. Goforth writes about place and belonging fearlessly."

—**Meagan Lucas**, author of the Anthony-nominated collection *Here in the Dark* and Editor-in-Chief of *Reckon Review*

T0343003

ANCHORED

ANCHORED

STORIES

KATY GOFORTH

Fort Smith, Arkansas

ANCHORED
© 2025 by Katy Goforth

Cover image: Getty Images via Canva Pro License

Edited by Casie Dodd
Design & typography by Belle Point Press

Belle Point Press, LLC
Fort Smith, Arkansas
bellepointpress.com
editor@bellepointpress.com

Find Belle Point Press
on Facebook, Substack,
and Instagram (@bellepointpress)

Printed in the United States of America

29 28 27 26 25   1 2 3 4 5

Library of Congress Control Number: 2024950523

ISBN: 978-1-960215-32-1

ANCH/BPP42

To Alex. You are my home.

Contents

My Diesel Ghost

Daddy was a diesel ghost, floating into my room in the middle of the night and leaving a soft-edged memory in my dreams. The crispness of his shirt sleeve rubbed against my neck as he bent down to give me a goodnight kiss. No matter that I had been tucked in hours before.

Outside my window, the Duke Power streetlight lit my tiny bedroom, giving me just enough light for me to barely part my lashes and take a peep. Daddy lingered, giving my leg a few extra squeezes through the quilt. I'd quickly close my narrow view in the hopes he didn't realize I was awake.

Lemon oil mingled and danced with the diesel fumes, shoving its way through my bedroom door left ajar. This meant Mama was up too. No surprise. Mama said after midnight, with the house at peace, was the only time of day to clean.

The stories from the road clung to Daddy, saturating him with mystique and adventure. Then they would drip dry off, leaving their marks on my still-developing brain. Sure I wasn't going to be jostled awake, I would feel Daddy sink into the edge of the bed, making it sag just like Mama always told me not to do.

"Don't you break down the edge of that bed," she'd say with her eyes transforming into angry slits.

I'd fight the urge to open my eyes, sit up, and throw my

arms around Daddy. He was closest to you when he thought you weren't looking. As he shifted his body to let loose the tightness from ten-hour-plus days in a big rig cab, the diesel fuel and his cologne fought to dominate the air around us. I tried to inhale deeply without alerting Daddy. I let the scent overtake and lull me back to my dreams.

J. Chisholm-boot impressions would greet me the next morning—heels still visible in my plush harvest-gold carpet. The edge of the bed where Daddy had sat left the faint evidence of his presence where the quilt had been flipped over to expose the plain backing. Throwing the quilt back, I'd swing my legs over the edge and slide down from the mattress, slipping my feet into the cowboy boot heel impressions from the wee hours of the morning. Inhaling deeply, I'd follow Daddy's now faint scent from my room, down the hall, and into the kitchen.

But I was too late. Daddy, my real road cowboy, had disappeared. All that was left was the faint scent of my diesel ghost.

Origami

The first time grief had a noise was when it escaped from my fifteen-year-old sister's body, a sharp exhale of air quickly followed by a slamming door.

The BellSouth rental phone pierced our Saturday afternoon. I stood in a doorway and observed as my mother's hand covered her mouth. Her head bobbing up and down as if the caller could see her.

With the receiver safely back in the cradle, she delivered the news. My sister's summer church camp crush was gone. No longer part of the world where I was watching the tragedy unfold.

The slamming of the door made the glass rattle in the panes and echo throughout the small ranch house, not quite shattered but still not whole.

My sister bolted for the driveway and crumpled on the asphalt full of July heat. Arms wrapped around her legs as she folded herself tight. Origami full of folded grief. I stood at the storm door pressing my face against the sun-soaked glass with the rest of my body tightening. A response to her grief.

My seven-year-old self now understood sympathy and empathy. Two lessons and only had to pay the price with one tragedy. Sobs filled with unwritten letters holding declarations of first love escaped my sister. So many firsts for her in just one day. I went to her.

I stood awkwardly in front of her with no words. Comfort was not a class taught in our home. You must suck it up. You should move on. You can't change the past. Tragedy is therapeutic, but only if you keep it to yourself.

I squatted down in front of her, hovering just outside of her hurt. Then I stretched my arms out, breaking the barrier between us. She folded her head tighter to try and contain her emotions, but I kept stretching. My short arms circled her the best they could.

Lessons Learned

The sound of waves sends uneasiness throughout my body, settling in my nerve endings and flicking them. Mix the sound with the smell of salt and marsh, and my body kicks on the turbo option zooming forward into my own anxiety. I would explore this with my therapist, but I know the origin.

Mama used to line up the live sand dollars on the splintered rail of the beach cottage. They were covered in a mossy gray. Alive and wondering where their wet home went.

She would put one in my hand so I could feel the tiny hairlike feet tickle my skin as if it were trying to read my lifeline and warn me of the future. She would snatch the sand dollar back from me, and I would be left with a yellowish stain. A signal from the creature that it was alive and needed water. An SOS in its own colorful language.

Marching up and down the deck, she would douse them with a mixture of water and Clorox. Her intention was to change them. Make them pure. Turn them into something she could display for others to envy. Mama didn't like much in its natural state.

I would watch her kill them, hanging over them with a smile and observing as her concoction ate their life away. The mossy gray would slowly turn to white. Some effort was required. Maybe a scrub to wash away the last vestiges of its wildness.

Mama would gingerly pick up the dead sand dollars with her blush-lacquered nails, cradling them close to her bosom as if they were preemie babies. She'd make them brittle. More likely to crumble under a touch. Once in a while, she would cradle one too tightly and the razor-thin edge would turn to dust. She would lob these over the deck railing into the sand dunes. Discarded for not being perfect.

A Polish Breakfast

I was drawn to kids that didn't look like me, talk like me, eat like me. You name it. If they were different, then I wanted to be friends. My mama says I was like that from the time I could walk and talk. Word was that a new girl was joining our class, and she was Polish.

When Paulina was introduced to our seventh-grade class, it was no surprise to my mama when I promptly asked if she could spend the night. Spending the night was the ultimate seal of a friendship. It meant you could stand each other's company for at least twelve hours. It didn't mean much about the parents trusting each other. If it meant our parents had a free Friday night, then they were shoving us off at the end of a stranger's driveway.

Paulina and I were fast friends. She didn't sound like me. I could draw out a vowel like it was the chorus of a song. When Paulina spoke, it was a performance with a staccato rhythm. I was mesmerized.

Breakfast at my house meant a hot meal. No cereal for us: That was reserved for a nighttime snack. Paulina would come over for an evening of watching Baby Houseman choose Johnny Castle over her uppity and judgmental dad. We would crash out on the den floor under a pile of quilts and pillows.

Sizzling hot sausage would tickle our noses and pull us from our sleep toward the kitchen. There we would find biscuits and molasses, eggs frying, and a gallon of orange juice sweating on the table. My new friend never asked me what anything was. She just dug in and happily chowed down with me.

After hanging at my house for weeks, Paulina invited me to hers. She explained that her family had been unpacking from the move, but her mom finally said it was a good time to have me over. Boy, I couldn't wait. If Paulina's mama talked like her, then it was going to be like Christmas.

Paulina and her mom came to pick me up. The compact car pulled into the driveway, but there was no driver. My mom and I were both stumped. I gathered up my overnight book and my bag (yes, I was that kid that had to read before I could go to bed), and we headed out to the driveway. When we peered into the car's driver side, there was a slip of a woman in the seat. She could barely see over the dash and was gripping the steering wheel with a soft confidence. She said her name was Anna, and I fell in love on the spot.

Even as a tween, I had some understanding of how overwhelming it must be to land in South Carolina with a different accent and traditions. We arrived at the duplex Paulina's family was renting until they found a house to put down roots.

Luck had found me again, and my excitement was shooting out of my face in a grin that couldn't be contained. We walked in, and I was greeted by artwork. And I'm not talking about a velvet painting of *The Last Supper*: Each piece had a small brass lamp mounted above to showcase the beauty. And there were more than paintings and framed pieces.

Richly colored and textured rugs hung over the banister of the catwalk above our heads nestled into the pitched ceiling. Real leather furniture was expertly arranged in the living room, and some sort of stark white rug in an animal hide I couldn't place tied the small room together. It made me feel fancy yet invited to explore and relax. I had never experienced anything like this. My house had the requisite La-Z-Boy that sat in the center of the living room in front of the television: Good luck getting a peek around it from the navy flowered love seat set directly behind it.

Paulina and I did the typical things tweens do when they spend the night with each other. We watched a movie, and then spent half the night whispering to each other in the dark. Morning came fast, and I could hear a man's voice floating up from downstairs. I knew Paulina's dad traveled a lot for work. He must have appeared during the night just to disappear again. I tiptoed out of the room to find a bathroom and found myself standing on the catwalk able to peer down at a small dining table.

The smells hit me before her parents' words did. Aromatic breads, dark brown and some light colored and dotted with what appeared to be raisins loaded one side of the table, along with some sort of dark red jelly or preserve. Then the smell of sausage hit me and drew me to my knees, so I settled in and spied from above. Finally, I realized they weren't speaking any language I had ever heard, but it was like listening to an orchestra for the first time. Made me feel refined even if I wasn't sure what the words meant.

I took care of my business and slipped back into Paulina's

room. She hadn't moved. I whispered, "I saw your mom and dad having breakfast." My stomach rumbled. I wanted to taste that breakfast. I wanted to sit at the table and take in the conversation like a symphony. Paulina rolled over without opening her eyes and said, "We will have late breakfast." That was it. Nothing else. I lay there on her trundle bed and wondered if that raisin-studded bread would make an appearance at late breakfast.

Later that morning, we were sprawled out on those fancy leather sofas with our legs up in the air resting on the back of the couch. The television was our company. I could hear Miss Anna bumping around the small kitchen. I had seen eggs on the counter and some orange juice. The small table was spread with a crisp white tablecloth, and real cloth napkins were arranged next to gold-rimmed petite plates. It looked like fine dining for late breakfast.

We were called to the table and settled in, still clad in our pajamas. The table was neat and not cluttered. A loaf of already sliced bread was displayed on a serving tray. Next to the tray were a variety of small bowls filled with so many treasures. One had radishes. The next held small tomato slices. Then came sliced cucumbers and finally a bowl filled with what appeared to be egg salad sprinkled with chives. The dark red jelly had made an appearance at late breakfast, and I couldn't take my eyes off it. Paulina spotted me and said, "It's plum jam. It's good. Make a sandwich."

I watched as she laid some radishes and tomato slices on her bread. Next came a generous spread of the egg salad and chives topped off with a cucumber. Not knowing what else to do, I followed her direction and made my own open-faced breakfast sandwich.

But late breakfast wasn't over yet. Miss Anna began to clear some of the small dishes from the table and replace them with fresh ones. There were a variety of jams, including the plum. But now there was a chocolate spread, which I would later find out was Nutella, along with butter, sugar, and honey. We were having dessert breakfast.

I was fully on board.

◊ ◊ ◊

I make my own breakfast now. Some mornings consist of me shoving a protein bar in my tote bag, only to be forgotten in the chaos of starting the day. Other mornings consist of sitting down in front of my laptop empty-handed, breakfast a long-forgotten memory.

But then the weekend appears and presents the opportunity to slow down. I slip two pieces of locally made sourdough into the toaster. I coax the eggs in my cast iron skillet to cook just right and leave a runny center. Settling into my breakfast table, set with my favorite Corelle Butterfly Gold dishes, I spread the cloth napkin over my lap. Then I reach for the plum jam.

Francine Pascal Goes
to Bible Camp

I hoisted my eleven-year-old self into the passenger van with *Baptist Church* running down the side in blue vinyl letters. My mom had unloaded my duffel bag and left it in a pile at the back of the van. Someone's dad was supervising the stacking and shoving of our camp gear. We were off for a week-long adventure at Bible camp in Fairfield County, South Carolina.

I hugged my tote bag full of chewing gum and books close to my body. A body bursting like the buds on a plant at the first hint of spring. I was so uncomfortable. My mom said I had to go. She told me to give it a chance. I asked, "So, I can call you and come home if I don't like it?" She snorted. "No. You're going for the week. But you will like it."

Long tanned fingers pulled at my T-shirt through the window. "Have fun. I'll be here at the end of the week." I nodded at my mom and gave her a half smile. It's not like I had any other choices.

With a heavy sigh and an eye roll for extra drama, I pulled out one of my books: Sweet Valley High Book 18 *Head Over Heels*. My mom had just bought it for me, so I hadn't even smelled the newness of the pages yet.

Folding myself into a tight ball so I didn't touch the girl next to me, I opened the pages and my shoulders let loose. Books calmed me. They were my friends. I had rushed through books 16 and 17 to get to this Francine Pascal story. *Head Over Heels* featured a main female character that was deaf. While I wasn't completely deaf, I was close to it. By 11 years old, I'd had numerous surgeries to try and restore some of my hearing. There had been moderate success, but I still mainly read lips.

It was a rare treat to find a character that was like me. There was a tap on the front of my book. I barely lowered it to see who was bothering me. Mrs. B was turned around in her seat and giving me one of those stares that some adults give kids. It's like they already know what they're going to say is bullshit, but they're an adult so you have to do what they say. We hadn't even made it out of the parking lot yet, and this woman was bothering the only quiet kid with a book.

"Where did you get that?"

I thought of so many snotty answers to this question. I got it at our local Waldenbooks. Where else would I get it? Feeling a tiny bit sorry for this woman's daughter, I lowered my book.

"My mom just bought it for me."

Mrs. B pulled back from me and clutched her non-existent pearls.

"Your mother bought you that? With that boy and girl on the cover? I find that hard to believe."

Now I sat with this last sentence for a good thirty seconds. I was puzzled. Why would my mom not buy me a book? Bruce Patman and Regina Morrow were hugging on the cover. It was a Baptist church, sure, but hugging wasn't frowned upon. It wasn't connecting for me, and I was annoyed she wouldn't leave me alone.

I marked my place in my book with my lucky bookmark because it was clear this wasn't going to be a fast conversation.

"Well, she did."

I stared at Mrs. B with an equal amount of distrust and respect. She was an adult in charge, after all.

"I'll just take that for now."

Mrs. B pulled my book from my hands. I pulled back slightly, and then thought better of it.

"I want to call my mom from the church office."

"You can call her when we arrive at camp. I'll talk to her too. I want to make sure she knows what you are reading."

The respect I felt obligated to give Mrs. B seconds earlier had disappeared. Now I was angry and upset. She took my book, which was a comfort tool for me. A book allowed me to escape any awkward conversations with the other girls. It let everyone know I was busy and not interested in how the Dr Pepper Lip Smackers made you look like you were wearing lipstick.

The two-hour drive churned up everything inside of me, both emotions and my actual guts. I was a mess. I was already nervous about meeting new people and trying to explain when I couldn't hear them. Reading was my escape from feeling like I didn't belong, and now my book had been taken away. I had more in my tote bag, but I wasn't about to let Mrs. B get her hands on them.

We arrived, and the mosquitoes carried me to my cabin.

I grabbed a top bunk and spread my sleeping bag out on the thin mattress. I stashed my tote bag full of books near the top and put my pillow over that. I wasn't taking any chances.

The teen counselors descended upon us with a cheer about Jesus dying for us and taking our place. It was peppy. I clapped but didn't offer a smile. I was still upset with Mrs. B and hadn't forgotten about my promised phone call home.

Later that evening, after our group had met with our counselors and gone over the rules for the week, it was our age group's turn to make as much racket as we could in the cafeteria. There was Hi-C pink lemonade available, and this did start to cheer me up. As I chowed down on my small square of room-temperature lasagna, I looked around for Mrs. B. I spotted her near the back of the cafeteria with the other chaperones and her daughter.

Mrs. B's daughter was cool. She didn't seem to like her mom's judgment any more than I did. Before making my way over to Mrs. B, I looked around for the first aid station. During our rundown of the rules, our counselors had told us the first aid station was in the cafeteria. There was an actual nurse on duty. My plan was coming together.

I got up and delivered my tray and dirty dishes to the cleaning station. Then I made my way over to Mrs. B.

"I don't feel well."

Mrs. B patted at her lips and inhaled deeply. I suppose she'd had about as much of me as I had of her.

"What's wrong?"

I had given this next part some thought. I didn't want

an upset tummy. That was the telltale sign of an amateur liar. My ailment needed to be something that couldn't be refuted while also making Mrs. B uncomfortable.

"I started my period. I need something for the cramps."

Mrs. B's hand fluttered near her neckline.

"You are 11 years old. What do you mean?"

I shrugged, "I don't know what to tell you. I have my period. Do you want to see?"

I knew she wouldn't call my bluff. She gathered up her things and led me over to the first aid station. She explained to the nurse that I had my period and was complaining of cramps. Only Mrs. B called it my "time of the month." She couldn't even say "period."

The nurse explained that she could give me some Midol, but she would need to call my mom for permission. Bingo.

The nurse handed me the receiver, and she dialed the long-distance code to get me connected. My mom answered on the third ring. As soon as she said hello, I went for it.

"Mama, Mrs. B took my Sweet Valley High book away from me on the van and won't give it back until you say it's ok."

My mom didn't suffer fools gladly, and I happened to know she didn't like Mrs. B. She also loathed when adults would call telling her whatever it was they thought I had done wrong, only to find out I hadn't done anything that wasn't allowed.

In a clipped tone my mom said, "Put her on the phone."

My mom's voice shot through the receiver piercing the heavy summer air in the first aid station.

"Give my child her book back. It's not up to you what she

reads. Don't make me come up there and take it from you. I have a job and don't want to waste the time. Now put my child back on the phone."

Mrs. B's hand was fluttering closer to her face that was hot with embarrassment and shock. She handed the phone back to me.

"She's going to give you the book back. You let me know if she doesn't. Now try to have fun."

I told my mom goodbye. The nurse, Mrs. B, and I all stood there in silence as the cafeteria began emptying out for the evening.

The nurse cleared her throat and asked, "I don't suppose you need anything for your cramps after all?"

I shook my head no. Mrs. B and I walked back to our bunkhouse in more silence. Before we went back in the bunkhouse, she pulled on my arm.

"You are not the adult in this situation. Do you understand that?"

My heart rose into my throat, but I nodded that I understood.

"You could have asked me to call your mom to get your book back."

Liar: I knew better. I also knew better than to call Mrs. B a liar because no matter how much my mom disliked her, she would not have her kid out in the world calling adults liars. Mrs. B put her hand on the small of my back, and we walked toward the bunkhouse.

I got my book back that night. As I snuggled down deep in my sleeping bag with boxes of Crayola crayons printed all over it, I knew things were shifting. I was still a kid, but I was also something else. There were all these expectations of me—to be agreeable, presentable, and likeable. It wasn't that those things were necessarily bad, but I wanted more. Whatever more was at eleven years old.

I finished *Head Over Heels*. I ended up being disappointed that Regina Morrow, the deaf character, managed to somehow read the lips of characters she wasn't even looking at. Being a hard-of-hearing person that relied heavily on reading lips, I knew this didn't happen. She was also faced with staying in Sweet Valley with her new love or going to Switzerland for a year and potentially having her hearing restored by a famous surgeon.

The idea that a young woman would struggle between choosing a high school boyfriend or having her hearing possibly restored fell flat for my eleven-year-old brain. I had questions: Why was this the choice? Why was it so hard to believe that someone wanted a relationship with a character with a disability? And the biggest theme that kept nagging at me was that somehow Regina Morrow was broken and needed to be fixed. After all of the drama and trouble, my book had let me down.

I didn't want to be at this camp. I didn't want to take orders from Mrs. B. But it wasn't a total loss that summer. I made some new friends. I walked to the swimming pool with my bunkmates yelling, "I said a Boom Chicka Boom," all in unison. And I managed to get to Book 19, *Showdown*, which featured Jessica Wakefield and Lila Fowler at odds on the cover. I knew Mrs. B would leave this one alone.

Becoming Linda

Linda was a princess dipped in acid-washed denim with her frosted lips and ink-lined eyes. To be in her presence was to be loved.

My mother was the first of us to become Linda's. Best friends. Hooked her at first sight. So many similarities: two little kids. Spouses always absent. Hours spent decompressing in the sunshine trying to let the heat burn through the ties their husbands had bound them with.

Ties that Linda's beauty hid well. Locked away tight in the pit of her perfectly flat stomach. Eyes set like topaz jewels masking the truth. No one with skin like bronze had troubles. No, not Linda.

You see, I became Linda's too. As a small child, I would steal the coveted seat that was her lap and snuggle into her open embrace. Moving her sparkling bangle bracelets up and down her arm creating a love song from her to me. Clinking and clanking in harmony. Looking up at her smile to find those two front teeth turned slightly toward each other in a kiss—an unintentional gift to us from Linda's maker. She gave love that knew no bounds.

Revlon's Charlie and the hint of coconut tanning oil would dance around her hair, mixing with a halo of smoke from her Kool 100s with the long filters. Pure glamour. Since we couldn't be Linda, we stayed close in the hopes of any piece of her attaching itself to us.

That's all Linda wanted us to feel. But there was more, and you could catch it if you were quick enough.

But I wasn't quick at seven years old. I saw it much later. As an adult, I studied Linda so closely I became a student majoring in tortured beauty.

Ink-lined eyes were ever so smudged and smeared. Shadows danced underneath the concealer on her face. Lurking under the shadows, something even darker than the bruises brewed. Slender bronzed arms bore someone else's fingerprints. Red marks from the grip had started to fade, yet the memory was still burning inside Linda.

Much like the bruises on her body, Linda gradually faded from our lives. The phone stopped ringing with invites to the pool. No more laughs with Linda. No more embraces. The thin veil softening the abuse to outsiders had slipped. She couldn't risk us staring at the truth, so she disappeared.

The truth first surfaced in the local newspaper: black ink searing itself into the minds of Linda's friends and community. That husband, her captor, was behind bars. But he wasn't put there because of his abuse of Linda. The locals called it white collar crime. Not as shameful so to spare him.

We continued to love Linda from afar, as close as she would let us.

Years rolled on with no sight of Linda. Then one day, in our local CVS, I caught a whiff—Revlon's Charlie now replaced with a citrus scent. A scent with a smile. It mixed with the leftover smoke from a pack of Kool 100s with the long filters. It was Linda.

There she was. Acid-wash denim replaced with flare-leg

dark wash for miles. Frosted lips now a respectable nude cream. Ink-lined eyes fresh and bright. Smile untouched with those two front teeth still turned slightly toward each other in a kiss.

Arms open, waiting on my body to pull it close to her and take me back to the love I felt as a child. Only this was better. Brighter.

Her sparkling bangle bracelets clinking and clanking up and down her arm with that same love song from her to me as she whispered, "How have you been, darling?"

We tried to cover a decade of happenings in a few minutes—impossible and yet still attempting. Linda gave me one last hug before the automatic doors opened, and she disappeared once again.

I roamed the aisles, not ready to leave. I found the fragrance aisle, and my eyes settled on a bottle of Revlon's Charlie. Yes, this is what I needed. Now I could visit Linda anytime I wanted.

That Time Strom Thurmond Almost Ruined My Family Day

A Saturday with Daddy, Mama, and Sissy was rare. Daddy was a real road cowboy, riding the interstates instead of bucking bulls. Mama was either cleaning the house or performing her financial wizardry on our blue-collar budget. Sissy's job was to entertain me. She would get down on the floor and balance my soft toddler belly on her feet to play the game she lovingly called "Airplane." Or she would play old church hymns on the piano, so I could pretend to be a famous dancer scooting across our harvest-gold carpet complete with a sculpted flower design.

But once a month, a rare Saturday would bring us all together with no interstates, no cleaning, and no entertaining responsibilities. First order of business was getting everyone in the car. This involved Daddy grumbling, "Get in the goddamn car," exactly five times before we would all get our goddamn selves into the car. Sissy would be last. Sometimes she landed in the back seat with only one eye done up with eyeshadow. Daddy didn't care. He had a plan and a schedule for the day.

First stop was the Thunderbird Flea Market. It was a veritable circus for oddities and curiosities. But my favorite part was getting to pet a chicken. So many chickens in cages, just waiting on my chubby hands to pet them.

And if you were lucky, sometimes there would be a dog to pet, too.

Daddy and Mama were on the hunt for antiques. Daddy liked glass, and Mama searched for blue enamelware. But the real draw was the food. It was an exotic market slapped right down in the middle of Spartanburg, South Carolina. Immigrants cooked foods from around the world: meat cooked on a stick and shaved off in front of you, fruits with seeds inside you could eat, and so many types of Vietnamese Bánh Cam—deep-fried, sesame seed-covered buns stuffed with eggs and a sweet, sticky sauce. Sissy and I were in food heaven, but we were just getting started. The food at the flea market was our amuse-bouche before the main event.

Daddy's signal that it was time to go was when I would cross my legs and whine that I wasn't going to pee in that port-a-potty. We would pile back into the car and head off to our next destination. And boy was it a good one. I would smell the french-fried onions before we'd even made it to the parking lot. We were heading to the Beacon.

The Beacon Drive-In opened in 1946, and it is so famous that there's a billboard out in California telling you how many miles you are from a chili-cheese a-plenty and world-famous Southern-style sweet tea. But the best part for me was Mr. J.C. Stroble—an Arkwright native and the South's ambassador of fried food. He took your order, and he took it as soon as your foot crossed over the threshold.

Mr. J.C. would yell out, "Call it!"

Daddy would say, "That's your signal. Tell him what you want, baby."

I prided myself on being fast and efficient, so as not to slow down Mr. J.C.'s line. And as soon as the words "cheeseburger a-plenty plain" (a burger buried under onion rings and french fries) would leave my lips, Mr. J.C. would shout it back to the kitchen in his famous drawl. It was magic.

One other thing the Beacon was famous for was being political. If it was an election season, then there might be an old white guy plastered across your Styrofoam cup in the hopes you'd remember that name when you were in the voting booth. Daddy hated this.

After we'd place our order, Mama, Sissy, and I would hold our breath until we shuffled down toward the sweet tea service. This is where all those Styrofoam cups were lined up loaded with shaved ice and waiting to be poured full of sugary goodness.

One Saturday we shuffled down, and there was Mr. Strom Thurmond staring back at us from those damn cups. Mama froze; she made no sound. I was little, but I understood that someone had to save this day. We couldn't let a rare Saturday be wasted, especially because of some old politician. Daddy had already snagged us a table, so he hadn't seen the cups yet.

I watched with wide eyes as Sissy grabbed the sweet teas and ferried them to the condiments and napkin station. Mama and I followed closely as if we were shielding Daddy from the sight of Strom Thurmond himself. My eyes followed Sissy as she asked the cashier for an ink pen. She took that pen to Strom Thurmond's face, and the next thing Mama and I knew we were staring at the devil himself. She'd given him some horns, a goatee—even a pointy tail and a pitchfork. Pure artistry.

Mama and I both clapped our hands, giving her drawing the applause it deserved. Sissy carefully placed the teas on the tray with the faces pointed toward her. She set down the tray on the table, and before she could deliver to Daddy his specially doctored cup of sweet tea, he grabbed another, with Strom Thurmond's unadorned face on it.

"Goddamn it! I don't want to drink out of a cup with him on it!"

Sissy quickly took the tea from Daddy's hand and replaced it with her doctored-up version of old Strom. Something tugged at the sides of Daddy's mouth—almost like his mustache was tickling him or something. Then he threw his head back and a belly laugh escaped. Sissy had saved our Saturday.

Restless

want to hear the music building to a crescendo in the theme song of *The Young and the Restless*. My stubby eight-year-old legs propel me toward the Naugahyde sofa. Maw's soft arms specked with bits of dirt from her garden are waiting on my soft landing. Cold breakfast biscuits arranged on the coffee table. The smooth "good brand" peanut butter oozing out the sides, just like I ordered.

My arrival is greeted by Maw's grin pushing her glasses up against her eyebrows—pure joy. She yells out, "Come on, Lou baby. Our stories are coming on." I smell the breakfast sausage on her hands clinging to them like a soothing salve.

It's 12:00 p.m., and the Burton Dixie Mill whistle blows. Lunchtime. Paw has a short commute before joining us. These are his stories too. The violin breaks through the tinny television speaker signaling we are close to watching the sixty minutes of drama unfold.

A whoosh of sticky air takes over the room. Paw's home. I didn't know then how tired fifty-five can be, but I understand it now. He wipes his feet on the bath towel placed by the door—a stand-in for a regular floor mat. As he bends to take his dirty shoes off, bits of lint cling to his silver curls. He runs his hands over the curls as Maw yells out, "Over the bath towel!"

I snuggle in tighter to her soft nook, trying to soak her in. Save her for later even though I don't understand later just yet.

But now, decades have passed, and I understand saving her for later. I understand the hurt from the realization that the soft nook fades. The breakfast sausage smell is no longer. And the Burton Dixie Mill whistle has fallen silent.

But I search YouTube for *The Young and the Restless* theme song. The tinkling of the piano keys begins, and my body softens against my chair, searching for my Maw's comfort. My tears flow down my cheeks and puddle in my collarbone. Full sobs.

Tomorrow I will go see her and search the rows of gravestones until I find my own last name staring back at me. A last name I hold so closely that I told my partner I refuse to give it up. The name connects me to her. Tethers me to my people. The people I come from. The people who sound like me. The people who smell like me. The people who still love me even when not in this world.

A Night Out with Big Ricky

Big Ricky wasn't my actual dad, but he was what I had. My mom had married him in a rush and divorced him in a rage. But Big Ricky still loved me like I belonged to him. Said I reminded him of all my mom's good parts. When he had a few hours off from driving his rig up and down the interstates, he chose to spend those hours with me.

Freshly popped popcorn and cigarettes mingled together, a comforting cocoon. The smells ignited my excitement. Big Ricky was home, and that meant one thing: an evening spent in the basement of the Spartanburg Memorial Auditorium coated in the sweat and swagger of the finest entertainers in the Southeast. The wrestlers of the National Wrestling Alliance.

We had a ritual on the two Saturday nights a month I spent with Big Ricky. I would stand in line for the tickets, and he would stand in line at the geedunk. This is what Big Ricky called the concession stand. I would secure two general admission tickets, and he would order eight hot dogs and two large gulps.

Those hot dogs would be fully dressed in chili, slaw, mustard, and onions and placed back in their original bag for safekeeping. Me and Big Ricky would get settled on the bench six rows from the bottom. Six rows was the ideal place to be able to see the action in the ring and be part of it when it left the ring: just close enough to spit at the talent or be spit on.

Big Ricky rested the bun bag on his meaty forearm and doled out a chili-soaked dog for me. The wrestlers no one knew, the no-names, burst into the ring with music blaring and fringe flying. I whooped and hollered, my mouth full of meat, chili, and slaw. A smear of mustard already run across my Dusty Rhodes T-shirt. It was magic.

The real action took place to the side of the ring. Sharp-dressed men in pressed suits held slim microphones to the lips of some of the greatest. The interviews and promos were taped here, and Big Ricky had us a special in on account of him knowing one of the camera guys. We would hustle over to a VIP area during a break between the no-name matches and the main events. I was so close to Ric Flair that I could still see the Aqua Net drying on his bleached mane. Witnessing his promos was like going to school for trash talk.

The night didn't wind down—it amped up. Big Ricky would hand out the second round of hot dogs, and I'd have just enough drink left to wash them down. With my energy replenished, I was up on my feet for the finale. The big match.

Big Ricky picked me up and plopped me back down on the end—giving up his prime spot to get me closer to the action. The Four Horsemen would amble up to the ropes with so much confidence that it oozed out of every pore. You could smell it from our seats.

My Dusty Rhodes T-shirt hung right at my knees and draped more like a nightshirt, but I paid no bother. He was my favorite on account of his accent and his lisp. Didn't slow him down none. Just made him unique. A standout from the others. A star.

Dusty Rhodes would mosey out next. The common man's wrestler. He knew exactly how the rest of us lived. You not only heard his words, but you felt them. Dusty looked like the rest of us too—belly peeking over his wrestling shorts and three chins when he grinned.

Chairs and bodies sailed through the air. The match left the ring, and I was in on the action in my prime spot. One of the Four Horsemen picked up what was left of my big gulp and bathed the crowd with it.

When it was time to go home, Big Ricky would drop me off in the driveway. He wouldn't come in.

He'd say, "See you in two weeks, Pudge." I couldn't wait.

The Ballad of Sugar and Doo

I smell the Pacolet River seeping through the screened porch. Trash and chemicals from the textile mills dump into Lawson's Creek and take a ride down to the river. My nose stings with the mix of Mother Nature and man's mess. I roll over, feeling the bite of the cold metal cot where my thin mattress rests.

"Sugar." Mama leans over the sink into the window to make sure her voice is heard. I look up to watch her lips. "Get on up."

Mama says I can sleep out here on the porch as long as she don't hear no complaining. My room is all pale peach walls with pink scarves draped over the lamps. It's a wonder there ain't been no fire. The ambiance is worth the possible tragedy. My older sister, Loraine, takes up the other half of the room. Come this time each summer, Loraine's body combines with the summer heat to shrink the space.

My cotton nightshirt sticks to my pale skin. My body is already a woman's, even if my mind still deals in races to the creek. Nature ain't fair like that. Course, there's twenty-two months between me and Loraine, but it stretches out more like a decade.

Her sophistication is that of a woman with her own kitchen and garden to tend. She mistakes my disdain for jealousy. I don't mind none. It keeps Loraine out of my hair and better yet out of my physical space. Besides, the hearing don't see the world the same.

I'm not completely deaf. In fact, Doc Whaler says, "Sugar, I think all the words go through your ears to your noggin. You just choose to process what you want." Then he laughs so hard he makes himself a whole 'nother chin.

When I was born, all those tiny ear bones people have were missing. With nothing for the words to bounce off, I couldn't hear. Mama didn't even notice until I went to proper school.

By then, I'd learned to read lips and had developed my signature monotonal response to about everything. No one ever bothered to ask if I was uninterested or if I couldn't hear. Three surgeries and years spent back and forth on the road to the fancy doctor in Atlanta, and I could hear some. My life is not much different for it.

I'm on the cusp of sixteen and sleeping on my mama's porch, where a stranger would be hard-pressed to find one speck of pollen. The sun has long since been up, which means Daddy has been working on at least a mile or so of road. Daddy is in asphalt. That's how Mama says it.

"Joe is in asphalt," she says, as if she's holding a mint julep in a copper cup.

She don't pay no mind to Daddy coming home coated in layers of sweat, muck, and silvery black specks. Some of those black specks have become part of who Daddy is. Buried so deep in his skin they've meshed.

"Sugar," Mama says but adds a letter "h," so it comes out sounding like "Shuga."

"Sugar! Get on up and fold your sheets." She jostles the cot with her knee. She's so close to my face I can smell her cup of morning coffee.

I drag myself out of my own thoughts and from my slumber. I feel the vibration of a body throwing itself against the screen door.

"Doo boy! Where you been?"

I jump up to let my dog Doo in. He's sopping wet, probably been down to Lawson's Creek for a morning dip. It doesn't sound half bad in this humidity. Doo lowers himself to the wooden floor in one whomp, letting out all the air in his body as he puts his chin on my foot.

"I love you too, boy."

I pull the Emerson one-speaker jam box off the shelf that also holds some of Mama's canned green beans she's brought up from the cellar. The beans glisten in the morning sun like rare gemstones.

I hit rewind and let the cassette tape run all the way backwards. I can't miss one note from Ms. Lynn's mouth. The honesty of her words transforms to pure grit, which settles down in my soul for me to examine over and over again. Loraine says I alienate myself with music. She just hates I sit so close to the TV that I block her view.

I never miss a chance to watch Ms. Loretta Lynn sing on the TV. Her costumes overcome me, and I watch the words form on her lips, memorizing the shape of each one. She's my idol. Ain't no woman gonna take *her* man, that's for sure.

Loraine often catches me with my ear pressed up against

my Emerson jam box. Normally, I smell Loraine when she enters the room. Mostly, she smells like her White Shoulders perfume. As if Loraine is sophisticated enough for White Shoulders. She pokes fun at my singing. Poking fun at my speech problems I can't help. It's just the way I'm made.

But Doo loves my singing. Slaps his tail against the floor to applaud.

"Sugar! For the last time, fold up that mess!" Mama's face is red from irritation and the heat.

I pull the thin cotton sheet off the bed and let it drape over Doo. He doesn't stir a bit.

"Sugar Barlowe! I don't even know who you belong to at times." Mama storms out to the porch and pushes the screen door open, demanding that Doo leave.

I don't belong to no one. I'm Sugar Barlowe, the next Nashville singing sensation.

I'm swaying my head and hips to Jessi Colter sweetly telling me about storms never lasting when I hear the screen door ricochet against the frame. Someone is angry. I shove the rest of the sheets into the washer and dance my way toward the porch.

"Mama! Mama! That stupid dog has ruined my dress. Just look! It's covered in creek water and mud."

The shrieks are so loud that I peek around the corner to the porch. Loraine is standing there in a chambray shirt-dress with the entire front soaked and splotched with red mud. Doo is waiting patiently at the screen door as if someone should let him in to finish his masterpiece. Mama makes a beeline for Loraine and the dress.

"Oh, honey. We can't get this mud out in just a wash. What time are you supposed to meet the girls?"

Loraine and her girlfriends meet at Teggy Jackson's house all the time. What they do there I will never know. They treat it like some top-secret club, I suppose to make them feel more special than they really are. Loraine and Teggy are going to Wofford College come August. Gonna be roommates. Makes me gag.

Mama grabs Loraine's sun-kissed arm and drags her through the doorway toward the laundry room, shoving me out of the way. I'm used to being shoved to another spot. Don't belong to nobody in this house. Except for Doo boy.

I grab the Emerson and plop down on the naked mattress. I place my best ear next to the small speaker and lose myself in the vibrations. Daydreams overtake me and send me on adventures.

Tomorrow night, I'm going to slip off this porch and behind the wheel of Daddy's company truck. Doo boy will jump into the passenger seat, my co-pilot on this adventure.

A Glamorous Life

I was born old. My mama and daddy had been busy before me and stayed busy after me. I was number four of thirteen. Lucky in some ways. I got marked as Lettie. Number ten got left with Tibb. And, well, the last one just got saddled with the nickname Hump. We don't even know what his real name was.

I was fourteen years old when John Lee showed his face on Daddy's farm.

Mama said, "Lettie girl. You're a woman now. But just 'cause you're a woman don't mean I ain't your mama. Don't go to sassing me or thinking you get to run off with the next boy you see."

By fifteen, I'd married John Lee. He'd presented me with the most beautiful diamond. It was from the Jewels of Joy line. Not some five-and-dime ring like a few of my sisters had.

Mama worried but not enough to stop me. I think she was more worried she was losing an extra hip to ride one of her babies on. Daddy didn't say much. What could he say? He didn't have anything better to offer me.

Besides, John Lee was movie-star handsome. He had dark curls that fell across his forehead and blue eyes for days. He'd picked me—Lettie Ann Hill. My legs stuck together from my thighs to my knees, but John Lee loved me still.

Our first Valentine's Day together was something. John Lee had gone down to the drugstore and picked out a small pack of cards. They had hearts on them. Some were pale pink with roses. Others were blood red with sashes across the front declaring undying love to a one and only. I know what they all said because John Lee gave them all to me.

He said, "Lettie, I don't reckon I have anyone else I love like that, so you can have them all."

My own baby came when I was sixteen. Mae was an easy baby. I suppose just one baby is an easy baby after growing up with my crew. One day, not too long after Mae had arrived, John Lee came home with a wig form. He'd scratched my name on the bottom of it with his pocketknife.

He said, "Now go on to the salon and pick out some nice hair to make you feel good on Sunday mornings at church."

That's exactly what I did. I picked out a wig that matched my natural color just right but gave me some height and some extra curls.

I had to work. I got a job in the cotton mill right alongside my John Lee. Judee Mae Birdsong, a dear old neighbor lady who I loved so fiercely that I named my first baby after her, kept my Mae and then John Leonard once he came along a couple years after.

We lived in a two-room wooden house right by the train tracks. No floor. Just dirt. But you know what made that house special? It was mine. Didn't belong to no mill owner.

I'd stroll home with lint in my hair and sweat and dirt caked in any crease it could find on my already broken-down body. I'd see that Jewels of Joy wedding set sitting on the pine dresser right beside my wig form, holding all those curls that matched my hair just perfect. It was my glamorous life.

In the Garden

t was that time of year again. That time when the air would flip a switch from a humid soup during the day to a brisk chill overnight. But that was mountain air for you. It was that time when I would roam the garden in the backyard. I would start in the canning room, which had been added on by my Paw at some point in the sixties. Everyone praised him for building that special room for my Maw. I thought it was founded in selfishness. The man liked to eat.

In the summer of 1985, I was eight years old, and I thought it was the most exciting thing in my small world to go visit my grandparents for the weekend. After a restless night's sleep on the Naugahyde sofa—tossing and turning and sweating and sticking to it—I would start to stir at the noise of my Paw opening the door to the canning room. I'd slip off of the sofa and already feel the hint of the overnight chill leaving the room and the heat of the day closing in around me. No air conditioning in this house. After pulling on my prized Edwin P. Todd Elementary School tiger shirt and jamming my feet into my once white Keds, I would hurry to the back of the house toward the canning room.

Most of the time, my Paw would have already slipped out the back door of the canning room to his garden. And this is where the magic would start for me. Careful not to let the screen door slam and alert him to my presence, I would ease myself down the concrete steps and hurry toward the rows of corn. My hiding spot. By this time, I could catch him slowly walking the rows and rows of his bounty—tomatoes, beans, cantaloupe—and a few special rows of carrots just for me to pull before they were even ready. I can still hear his voice say, "Baby. Don't you pull those carrots before they're done cooking in the ground." And he would shake his head with the thick silver waves falling forward to rest on his Buddy Holly glasses. But I could hear his smile when he said it to me. It tickled him that I couldn't contain my excitement.

As I walk the rows now, you can see the signs of crow's feet starting on my face. My Paw is a memory in this garden. This is where he lives and creates still. Because you see the cantaloupe are from the seeds he so carefully cultivated all those years ago. The tomato, still green on the vine for now, is the special blend he played with in his greenhouse. Now it satisfies me on a summer sandwich coated in Duke's mayonnaise. I'll pick the beans when they're ready and prep them on the very porch he built for my Maw. Then they will be cooked down with a slab of fatback just as intended. And, of course, I'll pick the carrots before they are ready.

Paper Dolls

first learned about her while sitting in an Ingles grocery store parking lot. I was in town from college, and my mother needed to go to the store. She burst into tears and said, "You have another sister. I gave her up. Don't hate me." I thought about it for the few seconds I was given and responded, "I don't hate you. You had a baby. It's ok." Then we walked into Ingles and shopped. There was no family meeting. No handwritten letter pouring out her soul. We put the makings for dinner that night in our cart while she told me about 1966, her decision, and the baby that would change my life.

If an emotion wasn't beautiful to the outside world, then you didn't feel it in my Southern family. Only show the happy times. It was like being a paper doll—beautiful clothes for the world to see on the front but exposed on the backside with those beautiful clothes just barely hanging on by paper-thin tabs. You shoved unwanted emotion down deep inside of your belly to burn. It's what my mother had been taught before me, her mother before her, and so on. And it was very much like a fuel for me. As we walked the aisles and my mother shared her story, she also issued a stipulation. Rules for how to move forward with this new-found information. No talking about it. No talking with my friends, my family, and certainly not my immediate family. I felt my mother's shame wash over the entire cereal aisle that day. I was angry, and once again I would shove it down deep and just let it burn away. I was also interested. There was someone out there who might look like me.

I went back to college, and I sat with this information. There was no deep dive into an internet search at this time. It was the late nineties after all. I did the one thing I always did when I had information that I couldn't trust with anyone else around me: I called my big sister. She had actually been given a few more details about the baby—a name, a birthplace, a birthday. I also confided in a friend who I knew was adopted. Looking back on it, I realize this was my deep dive into the internet. For the first time in my young life, I was not accepting that Southern shame that women get labeled with so often, especially when sex is involved. My mother shouldn't be ashamed. All she did was have a baby. And this shouldn't bring shame on my family. It could be a joyous finding if I let it be.

I found comfort through the years talking to my friend about her adoption. I would daydream about finding the baby, but I could never move to the next stage of actually finding her. At this point in my life, I was newly married and teaching college English. I would sneak in writing prompts for my students that touched on adoption and its history in the South, but what I was really doing was finding excuses to search for more information. I knew my sister had been born in Charlotte, North Carolina, and she had been kept in the area until her adoption. I also knew it had been a private adoption, which could have meant that a religious organization was involved. So many complicated layers, but that burn deep inside of my belly had grown to a full-blown inferno.

In 2006, I sat outside of a Barnes and Noble waiting on the doors to open. Author Ann Fessler's *The Girls Who Went Away* had finally been released. Fessler gave a voice to young single American women who were forced to give up their children. She also shared her personal story of finding her own birth mother. I carried that book around with me like some carry Bibles. I wanted to know how my mother felt. I could have asked her, but I would work up the nerve and then hesitate too long. And to be fair, she owed no one an explanation. I knew that. So, I would continue reading and highlighting and making notes in the margins of Fessler's work. I was still no closer to finding the baby or unraveling what it would mean for my family if I ever did find her. I had started to understand the stigma and the shame that surrounded unplanned pregnancies, especially in the South. My home state of South Carolina passed the Safe Haven for Abandoned Babies Act: A mother can surrender her unharmed baby at designated safe locations without the fear of prosecution. When a mother does this, it's often picked up as a news story that details the baby's sex, weight, and measurements. The name of the law really says it all: *Abandoned Babies Act*. These mothers aren't abandoning their babies. They're making a conscious choice for the baby's safety. That's love.

It was the summer of 2018. That same friend who had talked to me about her adoption had been looking for her birth parents by using a DNA kit. She'd found them.

I quickly called my sister, and the story spilled out so fast that I didn't think about the repercussions. A month later I was standing in my kitchen keeping my husband company as he cooked supper, and I had a breathless and excited voicemail from my big sister. She and the baby had found each other. The fire in my belly that had pushed me forward turned into a big, heavy stone. I was terrified. In her message, my sister said she had an email exchange with Kelley. Kelley—the oldest of our trio now had a name. I scrolled through my email and opened the message. I frantically read it to my husband as he paused his cooking. My hands were shaking, and big silent tears were rolling down my cheeks. She had spent the early part of her life in North Carolina, but she had spent most of her life on the California coast. I was stunned. Being from the South and knowing that Kelley was born there, I just didn't expect her to be from the West Coast. I thought to myself, "Did she grow up with sweet tea? Did she shell peas with her granny on a porch? Does she say pecan correctly?" All of the emotion that I had been taught to stuff down deep had boiled over. I had imagined this moment since I was a young adult, but at no point had I thought past finding her. What do I do now?

My first emotion after finding Kelley was anger. Not anger at Kelley, but anger at the situation. It should be so simple. I wanted to know my sister; I knew who she was now. I should have a relationship with her. But the "what ifs" started to flood my mind. What if people thought less of my mom because she'd given a baby up for adoption? She had nothing to be ashamed of. I'm not even sure I would call it entirely her choice, but I knew how our small community would likely react. Social circles would shrink. Whispers at the church covered-dish suppers. Judgment of my mother and my family rather than the system that had been created to take these women's babies rather than offer the support needed to keep them. I chose to keep pushing through like I had on that fateful day in the Ingles parking lot.

Kelley and I emailed at first. These were long emails dotted with childhood and adult experiences we'd had. We dove deep from the beginning. This was when she shared that she was sick. Her condition was called Genetic Pulmonary Hypertension. I remember the day I told my husband this, and his face fell.

I asked, "What?"

He said, "Make plans to meet her now."

So we did. Next came the planning phone calls. A call from Kelley made me feel like I had been transported back to Thanksgiving feasts at my grandparents' house—cousins, siblings, grandchildren, and even friends all talking at once, and the noise being pierced frequently with genuine belly laughter. I learned about her childhood, raising her own children mostly as a single mom, and her love of animals and hairbows. She was never without her signature bow in her hair. Through our talks and emails, I learned that Kelley had been a paper doll, too. On the front side, everything was presented beautifully to the outside world, but if you flipped her over then you would get a glimpse of what she had pushed down deep inside to burn. Kelley raged against being a paper doll. That rage was inspiring to me. Calls from Kelley were familiar—a warmth. They were a piece of home.

We started to plan on her and her family coming to visit us in our hometown of Spartanburg, South Carolina. She wanted to see where we were from and where we grew up. My sister and I had assumed we would go to her because of her health, but she was insistent. She arrived with her husband and her youngest daughter in tow. We packed in visits to our favorite Spartanburg restaurants, Wade's and Papa Sam's. There was even a day trip to Charleston to explore Fort Sumter and get some fresh seafood. My mom was able to come with us. It was wonderful and sad to watch her take in that she was spending time with the baby that she last saw in 1966. These are memories that sustain me.

We lost Kelley on February 12, 2019. I was at work, and my phone rang. It was her husband. He told me she was very sick, and it was near the end. Twelve minutes later my phone rang again: She was gone. I knew Kelley was very sick, but I still hadn't planned on losing her. I sank to the floor of my office and all of that emotion I had proudly packed down deep just spilled out. My colleagues literally and figuratively lifted me off of the floor that day. As I was able to tell others what had happened, they too lifted me off of the floor. The judgment I had been worried about and the shame that still engulfed my mother perhaps didn't exist in my circle. No one was waiting to weaponize the story. They were simply sorry for my loss.

July 28, 2019 would have been Kelley's fifty-third birthday. Pushing against every emotion and anxious thought in my body, I planned a birthday celebration for Kelley along with my sister. We invited close friends that wanted to be on this journey with us and to support us. There was good food, good drink, and good company—all of the things that Kelley loved. We raised money in her name for the local humane society, and of course, everyone wore a hairbow.

This loss runs much deeper than people are ever willing to talk about—the loss of a sibling. There are so many layers to my relationship with Kelley. It started all those years ago in a grocery store parking lot. Had I caved to the small-town Southern societal norms that have traditionally been assigned to women, then I would have denied myself a relationship with my sister. I would have also missed out on knowing my mother on a different level. On a level that I could relate to myself as a grown woman living the small-town Southern life. I was no longer that paper doll.

Black Walnuts

Your mama is bred from a long line of black walnut trees. Tall and straight with a rich brown heartwood. Attractive and extremely durable.

When surrounded by others, her personality towers over them leaving no low branches to grab hold. Yet they stretch and reach with the hope of touching her leaves. Even grazing them with their fingertips.

If you watch her from afar, all alone, she will branch out closer to the ground, developing a personality that is tinged with sweetness but still leaving a bitterness. You might not even detect the bitterness until long after your encounter.

Her roots work the same as that black walnut tree. Taking hold so long ago and reaching into generation after generation after generation. Each mama exuding her juglone just like the black walnut. Inhibiting the growth of anyone around to limit competition. If you get close, she will stunt your growth, possibly even smother it. Emotionally stunt you forever.

But the black walnut tree can provide comfort. Mama can too. Growing fifty feet tall and stretching out beautiful foliage to provide shade and solace to others—those not coming directly from her body.

Fernlike leaves so light and airy. Light and air for those outsiders. They have taken nothing from her. Required nothing. For their reward, Mama's leaves turn bright yellow in autumn. A show.

But you are her fruit, dropping from her on a mid-October day. A love and hate relationship as you are made of a heaviness. You make a mess. She expels you. A nuisance encased in an ugly husk.

Some soul will come along and try to harvest you. Collect you. They will remove your husk immediately as to avoid you festering inside and molding. They will learn to wear gloves when handling you. Your stain, Mama's stain she has passed to you, leaving marks on anything that touches it.

You are hard at first. You will soften. Begin to rot. Perhaps this soul will step on your outside with an old pair of shoes, removing it to get to your sweetness. If unsuccessful, don't fret. Someone will come along and try again. Put you in a bucket and hose you down to remove any remaining husk.

You will have a decision to make. Let someone crack you with a hammer to get to your insides. Or become a black walnut tree yourself. Extending your roots and reaching into generation after generation after generation.

All That Glitters

Word around town is that my troubles started the day I killed a man. But that's not accurate. My troubles started when I was born here in Smyrna to a mama with a warped moral code and a ghost of a man.

The ghost, my daddy, died before I could even say his name. Mama said she tried to raise me up right. Each night at supper that summer—the summer that changed my life—Mama rattled on about our neighbor, Mr. Mullinax, panning for gold.

"Money is the root of all evil, and it is sitting in plain sight in his backyard. All that gold in that barrel. You spend all that time shoveling for him and get nothing. Nothing! He just hoards it all."

But money isn't the root of all evil. The love of it is. From where I was sitting at that supper table, I wasn't sure if Mama was mad at Mr. Mullinax for having all that money or just mad she didn't.

If she spent too much time on Mr. Mullinax not sharing his riches, then she'd squirm in her seat. Uncomfortable in her own greed. She'd say, "But now, don't go wishing for worms in another person's apple. Not right. I suppose I can't tell Mr. Mullinax what to do with his own money."

Mr. Mullinax was my friend. My only friend. I sat down by Wolf Creek and helped him collect his riches. We had us a routine. I would dig under the big rocks and inside the bends where the heaviest stuff settled. Mr. Mullinax would take my hard work and sift it looking for the riches. Then we'd walk back toward home where he'd promptly dump it all in a barrel behind his house.

Mama said it wasn't right—me doing all the hard work with the digging, and Mr. Mullinax taking it all. For a long time, I rolled my eyes at Mama's protests. But one summer day, things shifted inside me.

The musk of creek water filled our tiny kitchen. Mama recoiled from me as she put down my supper plate.

"Been making Mr. Mullinax rich again, huh? Doing all the hard work. You sure smell like hard work. Look like it too."

It felt like a rubber band slapped back against my heart. I did make Mr. Mullinax rich. Mama's protests had finally tainted my friendship. I started to doubt him.

On a Thursday afternoon, sun beating down and baking the sand like a pecan blondie, I killed Mr. Mullinax. I was digging and coated in sweat. He was bent over the creek bed wetting his bandana to cool off. As I brought the shovel down on the soft part of where his head meets his neck, I thought to myself, "I'm going to miss him."

I sat on the wet sand, my jeans absorbing the dampness. From both the exertion and shock, I was desperate for air. Taking it in so fast I choked on it.

As he fell, his head turned to look back at me. The shovel rested on Mr. Mullinax's cheek, covering his eyes. The realization that I had killed my only friend sped through my body with adrenaline.

I collected myself. My soaked jeans were weighed down by creek water. I lifted the shovel, and his clouded blue eyes stared back at me.

His arms were slippery in my wet hands. My biceps trembled with exhaustion as I dragged him off the sand and nestled him in amongst the wildflowers. I brushed my hand over his open eyes. I leaned back down and crossed his arms over his chest to signal he was at rest. This was all Mama's fault.

I was so lonely.

Smyrna isn't home to many. The sign into town says population forty-five, but someone will have to repaint that sign. With Mr. Mullinax laid out next to the creek, we are down to forty-four.

The sheriff found Mr. Mullinax resting in the wildflowers. Then the sheriff found me. Because of my age, I was sent off to a special hospital. Mama cried loud in the courtroom, making the sentencing more about her than anyone else.

Mr. Mullinax had a will. Turns out that barrel of gold was left to me—his good friend. Over a million dollars in gold right behind his old house.

Of course, all that treasure went to Mama.

I Am Shitty Bitty

I married Walt on the coldest day of the year. Family gathered around the dead oak tree in Mama and Daddy's backyard, overlooking the tobacco fields. Mama's eyes as cold as the temperature, signaling to me she understood the significance of the oak and the frigid day. My insides dying and cold as I took my vows.

Walt asked for my hand. Buck hadn't, so I said yes to Walt. Didn't know I had choices. Now they're both off to war, and I'm stuck at Mama and Daddy's house where the most exciting thing happening is fried chicken liver Sundays.

Everyone calls me Bit. Buck calls me Shitty Bitty. It drives my husband up the wall when he does, but I think it's funny. A term of endearment. I claim five feet, and I'm not. I have a tongue like an adder. That's where the shitty part comes from. I've earned it, so I claim it. Wear it like one of those patches they want you to be proud of in the Girl Scouts.

All I ever hear around here is criticism. Mama can't miss the opportunity to comment on how I look, as if my appearance is tied to her reputation. The house is a pressure cooker; Mama and I are gonna blow the lid.

When I can no longer bless Mama's heart, I check the mail. Buck writes me. Walt doesn't.

I have a ritual. I shove my feet in Mama's gardening clogs and fling the old screen door open with such force it slaps back with anger. Today, the hottest day in June the tobacco state has seen in years, my ritual is interrupted. With one foot on the top step and my arm out to catch the door, I see him. It's Buck. He's come home.

Our reunion scalds everyone close to us. I'm divorcing Walt. I say it out loud and eyes divert from my face to the ground as if divorce is a communicable disease. Mama says I can't divorce a man still at war and marry his friend. She coats me in her shame, but I am Teflon. I am Shitty Bitty.

I am no longer Mrs. Walt Houser. I am no longer Mrs. anyone. Mama says to marry Buck. I won't do it. Repeating the mistakes of the past is for the scared. I ain't scared.

Buck and I have adventures. When we have sex, I tell him what I want. I use my voice. My hands, not shy, guide him. We have passions upon passions upon passions. If our passion was gasoline, we would burn the house and the fields down.

Where others see flaws, Buck sees beauty. He blows the dust off my neglected parts and shines them up like new again. In the evenings, we sit on the porch—my feet propped on his knees and his hands working out my worries, putting me at ease through his touch.

Folks whisper still. But I don't care. I take risks. I broke one heart to ignite my own. I accept it. Because I am Shitty Bitty.

The Invisible Woman

She rummaged through the console of the ancient red Toyota Tercel. The paint used to shine like a forbidden apple. Now it was a dull pink and wearing in spots. She could relate.

No name tag. Must have left it on her dirty uniform. Damn it. She wasn't supposed to be working this shift anyway, but they always called her. They knew she would make herself available.

The heavy door swung into the alley, and the smell of old grease and fried onions instantly coated her. Not the perfume she chose, but it was the one she often wore. As she made her way back to the small break room, she stopped to clock in and check the board for her missing name tag. Most left them here, but she would end up halfway out to the parking lot before realizing hers was still attached to her.

Her eyes scanned the board with no luck. They settled at the bottom on a tag that said, "Mel." Lord, Mel was the old line cook and hadn't worked here in almost a year. Whatever. She would be Mel.

Her first table was a six top. Time to sparkle. The guys barely looked up from their phones to tell her what they wanted. She turned to take the order to the kitchen and heard two sharp snaps. One of them wanted her attention to change his order. Couldn't even call her Mel.

As she cleared the six top, the smell of Heinz 57 sauce hit her nostrils. It was smeared down the front of her uniform. Those university fellas were the worst. Like pigs bumping into each other at the trough, only pigs were smart.

Grabbing a wet rag from behind the counter, she worked at the brick-red stain. It spread out like the ugly watercolor portrait above her bed. She found it at the yard sales she frequented on her rare Saturday off. Her body felt like that painting. Discounted and unwanted.

Looking down at the table littered with half-eaten plates of hash browns scattered, smothered, and covered, she saw the bill with two pennies on top. Those sorry sacks of farts and too much confidence had stiffed her on the bill. Tipped her two damn pennies.

Her grandmother told her the worst thing about getting old was becoming invisible. She already felt like a ghost.

As she gathered the dirty plates and began preparing the table for the next set of diners, she heard someone clear his throat. She turned. Long, Wrangler-clad legs spread out in her path back to the kitchen. No. Just no. She yelled to the back, "Smoke break!"

The cool night nipped at her bare legs. As she rounded the corner to the alley, she spotted her: a raven-haired woman blowing smoke rings up above her head. She looked like an angel. There was a fresh tattoo on her bicep: Betty Boop as Rosie the Riveter. She gave her a tight-lipped smile.

She pulled her lighter from her apron, but there were no cigarettes. She knew where they were—right on top of the fridge at home. A hand touched her arm.

"Here you go. You look like you could use it. Take two." An offering from the raven-haired angel.

The touch felt like real electricity traveling from her arm all the way down to her lower belly. She blushed and nodded as she accepted the kindness. She lit her cigarette and took a deep inhale to calm herself. With her other hand, she smoothed down all of her flyaway hairs, and then let her hand continue traveling down her neck and hovering at her bosom.

Her words caught in her throat as she watched the woman flick the still-lit cigarette into the darkness. The woman made eye contact and flashed a wide smile. "I hope your night gets better, Mel."

And the raven-haired angel was gone, disappearing like the smoke rings above her head.

Grief's Watermark

For the longest time, I couldn't even say his name. The smell of pine trees would send me into the weird, dry parts of my brain where nothing of value could flourish. The stain of the day—the incident—spread throughout me and eventually began to fade. Edges of grief so faint others couldn't even detect. I sat down several times throughout the years to write about it. A therapist once told me it was the only way to move forward: face the grief and the trauma to get to the other side of it. My last attempt at taking this advice resulted in me thinking, "Ok. I will write, and I will face the grief." But I hadn't faced the loss of a lifelong partnership—or even more profound yet, the loss of a child. My grief didn't sound as tragic, so I still didn't write.

As a decade without Lee peeked around the corner, I tried to take this advice again. A decade can erode memories, leaving a flat place void of any ups and downs. As I sat down to write about my loss, I knew I could only do this if I stopped pretending. To stop pretending meant to not only face the loss again but to also recount the day. The memory had been double sealed and sent to the back of my mind. Shoved so far back it was forgotten and eventually covered in ice and of no use to anyone. So, I sat down to thaw my grief.

My close friend, Penny, had invited my husband and me to dinner to meet someone: "Anywhere you want to go."

"Who is he?" Her nervous fidgeting indicated there was more to the invite.

"He owns Anderson Arbor Pros. He climbs trees all day."

She had been at a pick-your-own strawberry patch with her daughter, and a man in overalls with three kids of his own in tow had approached her. Now I was being pressed to select a place to have dinner and meet this forward, strawberry-picking, tree-climbing dad of three. "Fine. We can go to the pub. If I'm going to be forced to meet a stranger, I can at least ply myself with fish and chips."

We went to dinner. I did not like him. From the time we walked to our table to the time we got up to go home, I thought he was cocky, loud, and told horrible jokes. The next day, my friend wanted to chat and break down the night before. I hesitantly voiced my observations, and she smiled. I decoded the smile in a flash. She didn't give a damn what I thought, even if she was asking. But she was my friend, and I cared about her, so I was going to give this loud, cocky, strawberry-picking stranger more chances.

Shortly after the dinner, dark times fell over my house. I had been diagnosed with cancer. My husband had been diagnosed with a rare autoimmune disease, and it was quickly winning. With no family close by and our pride in the way, we started to disintegrate like a wet newspaper breaking apart in a driveway. On a particularly hard day for both of us, we were trapped in our bed and starting to panic a bit about how things were going to get done. Not only did we need to work, but we had a house to take care of.

My husband heard the noise first. The shuffle of someone's work boots moving side to side all around the roof of the house. Next, the burst of gas-powered air. Someone was on the roof blowing all the leaves out of our overflowing gutters. It was the cocky, strawberry-picking stranger.

As the dark times continued to stretch before us, Lee became a bright spot. Turned out he lived close by and often worked in the area. Random texts would come through, summoning one of us to use all our energy to peel ourselves from our sick-couch position to answer the door. We were often greeted with groceries and enticing takeout meant to encourage us to eat. It didn't take long for Lee to understand we needed even more than an excellent Pad See Ew with a number two spice, and his deliveries started to include a visit. Days would stretch out before me and my husband when we might not see a soul, but Lee always made sure to punctuate the week at just the right time. He became more than my friend's love interest. He was my friend.

On an unseasonably warm April day, we made our way to Lee's house. It was a Sunday—and not one of those Sundays where you dread the looming Monday. I was firmly planted in the goodness of the day. One of Lee's kids had a birthday. We were greeted at the back door with offerings of cake. There were two kinds—one full of sugary goodness and one deemed the healthy version. He flashed a signature grin and said, "The healthy one tastes like shit." We visited and laughed. He talked about his three children and how they were growing up. The conversation was light. It would be the last time I saw him.

◊ ◊ ◊

I was sitting at my desk in the windowless office, and I considered ignoring the piercing ring of my office phone. Its demands bounced off my naked office walls. I stared at it until it stopped. I had moved into this new office and only a handful of people knew. I leaned over to look at the caller ID, and my cell phone began barking at me. It was the only ringtone my mostly deaf ears could hear. Pushing off the floor with my four-inch heels, I sailed across the office to my barking tote bag thinking, "What in the hell can be so important?"

I grabbed my phone, and before I could offer a greeting I heard, "I need you. I'm on Laurel Lane in Pendleton. Can you get here?" Penny's voice was filled with shaking fear, and my mind went straight to her young daughter. She interrupted my racing fears with, "It's Lee. He's fallen."

Scrawling down the address, I grabbed my keys and my bag. I popped my head in my officemate's door to tell her I had an emergency. She was concerned and wanted specifics. I waved around my scrap paper heavy with the address I hadn't even known existed a few minutes before. I wasn't making sense.

My officemate grabbed my shoulders and told me I should pull myself together if I was going to go help. Feeling like the real me was floating above my physical body I thought, "Yes, my friend has fallen out of a tree, but by God I will have no emotions." I refused her offer to come with me.

Laurel Lane was alive with blue and red lights. I eased my car up next to an officer and explained who I was. He shot his hand up, palm facing me, indicating I was not to move forward. A few minutes passed, and he waved me through. My stomach was up in my throat. I didn't want to be waved through. I couldn't do this.

Pulling my car off to the side of the road, I swung my legs out with my gold heels and close-fitted tomato-red dress indicating I didn't belong here. Emergency personnel and tree service employees swamped the area. Penny was nowhere in sight. I tapped the shoulder of a young man in a paramedic's uniform. "My friend called me and said there's been an accident. I need to see them both." He stared back at me, and I willed him not to say it. My eyes begged him to turn and ignore me—just leave it hanging in the air a bit longer. Don't say it and shift my friendship into past tense. But that's exactly what he did. "Ma'am, he's gone."

My legs stopped working. It felt like someone had slammed into me from behind, and I couldn't get any air. The young man's arms reached out to scoop me up before I hit the asphalt. The strawberry-picking father of three, not even near forty years old, was gone.

"He fell more than sixty feet from that pine tree. Was trying to top it. Your friend is in the garage across the street. News helicopters are all around, so someone took her over there for privacy." I nodded, still in shock. "Ma'am, it would be best if you didn't see him." The flood broke, and my tears came. I had rushed there thinking he was alive. Hurt, but alive. I didn't sign up for dead.

The young paramedic handed me a handkerchief. I cleaned my face and made my way across the street to the garage. Penny was sitting on the top step to a stranger's kitchen door. A woman came around from the back of the house to ask who I was. She was marching toward me with the determined speed of a seagull who had just sighted a piece of stale bread tossed on the beach. She was protecting Penny, and I was grateful. We sat in the garage in silence. Life had changed in the moment; we were sitting in between. Once we walked out of the safety of the garage, we would be in our post-Lee life. No rewind. No new memories. No more random deliveries of a Pad See Ew with a number two spice.

The first 48 hours piled up fast, packed with to-do lists. Still sick and at this point exhausted, I pushed through each task on fumes from my rage. The hardest task was standing by my friend's side as she told Lee's three children he was gone. The youngest, less than double digits at the time, crawled into my lap and wrapped himself around my neck. I tried to absorb all his fears. All his tears. But tragedy and grief don't work like that. They let you keep them close in your own body—ready to torment you at a moment's notice.

◊ ◊ ◊

The smell of fresh-cut pine trees triggers my flight response from the tragedy, pushing me toward bright memories like the last Sunday filled with chit chat and a shitty-tasting vegan cake. A year or more had passed when I had a dream. I say a dream, but I had drifted to an in-between state of light sleep with a soft-edged awareness of the room. Something pressed on my leg, so I rolled to my side, propping myself up on an elbow. He was there. There was no soft-lit ghost at the end of my bed. No spirit voice filling my ears. But I felt all the good parts of my friend in the room with me. He came to make sure we were okay. A visit.

We keep a picture of Lee in our entryway. Much like some people keep weapons in their bedside table, we keep his smile for protection—of us, the house, and anyone who enters it. We sit down with a good Pad See Ew number two spice and touch the grief. It leaves a watermark on you. A place where even if you can't see the delicate difference, you can feel the textured change. It's a reminder of an easy friendship. A friendship with no strings.

A pine forest is full of life. It's a lively place full of birds and mammals depending on the seeds and the bark for survival—the pine forest floor a thriving community. It's alive. When I smell a pine, I remind myself of these things. My mantra to ward off the panic from the grief. It's my way forward and a way not to fear the pines but welcome them, reminisce with them.

Welcome to the Starlite

Everyone has a limit. I hit mine on a picture-perfect Saturday in late April. I had resigned myself to being alone. Unlike my mother's generation, I didn't need a partner. I didn't need a marriage contract. I did fine on my own. Or so I thought.

The loneliness set in after I started perusing the online dating sites. It was as if knowing what my prospects were made it worse. My profile was overflowing with potential mates that had perfected the bathroom selfie. The few times I accepted a match I quickly realized the dating software had failed me. I had no gracious way out. My "thanks but no thanks" message was most often greeted with, "Whatever. You're an ugly bitch anyway."

But then I found Micah. Skin the color of a perfect cool inky night and eyes that gently urged me to give him my story. How had I stumbled upon this gem in the pile of patriotic T-shirts and scraggly beards? Micah was an open book. And a nice person.

Naturally, I started to get suspicious. I had been on the dating site for over six months before I met Micah. Nothing comes easy there.

After a hellish shift at the hospital, I was dragging myself into the door with a pile of mail. At the top of the pile was a postcard that read, "Welcome to the Starlite Inn: Where people can't help but be themselves."

I thought to myself, "What the hell? That's so weird?" But it caught my attention, so I threw it on the kitchen table rather than in the trash.

Two days later, I called the number on that postcard.

"Starlite Inn, where people can't help but be themselves." I was instantly lulled into a sense of trust and ease with whoever this velvet-throated voice belonged to.

"How can I help you today?"

I paused for a good five seconds. "Yes. I received this postcard in the mail a while back and thought I'd call and see what you have available."

"We were expecting you. So, will your friend also be joining us?"

I was stunned. How did they know I was bringing someone?

"There are no coincidences at the Starlite Inn."

Normally, I would have hung up the phone. But there was something so reassuring about the voice on the line. So on that picture-perfect Saturday in late April, Micah and I made our way up the Blue Ridge Mountains toward the Starlite Inn.

The drive wound us up the mountain to the point I thought I might be sick. When we left the main road for a gravel one, I was sick. The car bumped across the narrow gravel drive for what felt like a mile but was in reality much less. Just as I couldn't take the jostling anymore, the narrow drive opened to a small parking lot with a neat and simple motel high above. There couldn't have been more than six rooms connected to what looked like the office.

I shielded my eyes from the sun with my hand, and I could see into the glass wall. A slight man stared back at me, his pencil-thin mustache turned upwards with his grin. As he raised an arm to wave, my eyes adjusted to the sun, and I saw he was wearing a powder-blue tuxedo. Vintage perhaps. As if he was on his way to a very dated prom.

The man pushed the door to the office open with his hip and waved two plastic-looking motel key chains in the air.

"You made it! I do hope the drive was enjoyable."

He moved down the steep concrete steps as if he was floating. His fingers hovered above the railing, giving the illusion of a grip. When he reached the bottom, my eyes settled on his glistening white patent-leather dress shoes. Pristine.

"Do you need help with your bags?" The oddly dressed proprietor reached out and pressed the plastic key chains into my hands. "One for you and one for Micah. Just as requested." Then he gave me a wink. But I hadn't requested anything, although I was grateful for the separate rooms. I didn't know Micah all that well.

Micah turned to me curtly. "How does he know my name?"

"We know everything here at the Starlite. It's what makes us special. Well, and the internet. You can find out everything on there these days."

I watched Micah's face for any hint that I had been found out. Found out for what, I didn't know. But I felt a kinship with the tuxedo-wearing weirdo and wanted to smooth the situation over. Micah nodded and smiled.

"Very well. My name is Vincent. Let's get your retreat

started!" With that, Vincent tapped his watch twice. The sound was much louder than normal and almost ricocheted off the mountains. It was as if all other civilization held its breath.

Vincent looked over his shoulder. "Micah, grab those bags for you and the lady."

Without even acknowledging I was standing beside him, Micah said, "She can manage them herself." As soon as the words escaped his lips, shame washed over his face. "I'm so sorry. I don't know why I said that. Let me grab your bag."

Vincent placed his hand on my back. My shoulders instantly dropped from up around my ears and relaxed. "You are going to learn so much about Micah. The Starlite is the perfect getaway for a new couple."

We followed Micah up the steep concrete steps toward the Starlite. The building was old, but it almost glittered in the afternoon sun. Vincent held the heavy door for me, and Micah hustled in around me to be first. He dropped the bags in the middle of the room and sprawled out on the couch with his phone. The room was heavy with the scent of gardenias. I inhaled deeply, and the tension in my body melted.

"Your favorite, yes?" Vincent gave me one of his closed-mouth smiles, complete with a wink.

"Yes. My favorite." I wanted to ask how he knew, but the words didn't seem important.

I felt Micah's heaviness behind me. "Yeah. About that smell. It's giving me a headache. Can you open a door or something?"

I felt a puff of air escape Vincent's lips as he clicked his tongue in disapproval. He did not open the door. Instead, he turned my hand over and patted the two keys. "Make sure you give Micah room 217." I nodded.

"Cocktails and music begin at 6:00 here in the lobby. You will both be joining us."

He didn't ask. He told me, and I nodded. Because I wanted to join him. I needed to join. Micah bent down to grab his own bag and walked out, not even holding the door for me. As it slammed behind him, Vincent squeezed my arm.

"I'm so excited for the evening. Many things to come, my dear."

His joy was contagious. After such a hard ride here, my body had relaxed. I hated the word, but I felt renewed. Refreshed. I passed room 217. The door was closed, and the small window air conditioner was humming a sad tune trying to keep up with the weather. My room was next door. God, I hoped the walls weren't thin.

As I pushed the door open, a whoosh of chilled air greeted me. I felt movement behind me.

"Hey! Your room is nicer than mine. And colder. Let's trade." Micah had already scurried off before getting an answer. And he was back with his small duffel bag in hand.

"It's a trade!" He wiggled his plastic key chain at me before chucking it at my face.

I recoiled from the key and was in shock.

"Oh my god! Are you ok? I'm so sorry. I just thought you would catch it."

Rather than make the moment any more awkward, I left

Micah in the perfect sixty-seven-degree room. I peeked into room 217. The air felt like a wool sweater and smelled like vinegar.

"Oh, honey. No, no, no, no, no. Why are you in room 217?" Vincent was pissed.

"It's fine. Really."

He sighed heavily and tapped his watch two times.

"Life can be a rotten lottery, but you don't have to settle, dear. Choices abound!"

I heard Micah's air conditioner make a sad noise as it sputtered and stopped.

"Freshen up. Cocktail hour is just around the corner."

Washing my face with some cool water seemed to do the trick, although it didn't change the fact that my room smelled like a pickle factory. I knocked on Micah's door, but there was no answer. I took the short walk to cocktail hour alone and enjoyed the view of the Blue Ridge Mountains. Maybe this trip could still be saved.

"Hello there, dear." Vincent held the door open for me. "How about a cocktail for the lady? A pink squirrel. Yes, that's what you need."

Vincent handed me the creamy, pale pink drink, and I followed his eyes to the chair in the corner. Micah was in a serious and close conversation with a busty blonde. A busty blonde about ten years younger than me.

"Looks like he found a friend." Vincent patted my shoulder. "Rebecca came last weekend with her new beau. He left, but she stayed behind. If you open your eyes wide enough, the Starlite will reveal it all." He walked away swaying his body to Patsy Cline crooning about her sweet dreams.

Micah abandoned the blonde. "Hey. Is your AC working? The weirdest thing. Mine stopped about the time I got settled in my room."

The blonde was by his side. "Oh, have you met Rebecca?"

I nodded and moved away. I sipped my drink to try and soothe my frustration and embarrassment. I was wrong again. How did I keep finding these dead-end dates? I didn't want to be my mother. I didn't want to marry a man like my father. Yet here I was at the Starlite Inn watching my perfect-until-now boyfriend paw at a blonde.

Vincent sidled up to me and took me in his arms. We spun around the room, now to Ms. Kitty Wells telling me about living in Heartbreak U.S.A. It was almost as if we were floating just above the floor.

"You're going to be fine. Really. You will."

I pressed my cheek to Vincent's, and I felt it. I was going to be fine.

"There's so many of them out there. And when you find another, you bring him here. On the house. Vincent will take care of you. The Starlite will reveal all."

Our dance ended. Micah was still wrapped around the blonde. He didn't even know I existed.

I pushed the heavy glass door open just as Hank Williams began singing about your cheatin' heart telling on you. As the door closed behind me, the phone rang and I heard Vincent say, "Starlite Inn, where people can't help but be themselves." I looked over my shoulder and waved. Vincent winked.

Cherries in the Snow

The old neighbor lady passed on a hot Monday morning. No one found her until the Mobile Meals breakfasts and lunches stacked up against the screen door. Watching the house is my full-time job. Mama says to mind my business. Old neighbor lady house is my business.

No one's been back since her body was toted out in a black sack. I have urges when I watch the house. They pull at my stomach like a delicious ache. Mama says little gentlemen don't talk about their urges. One of them urges yanks at my insides and pulls me toward the back windows.

I take inventory of my surroundings. There's an old peach box propped up against the siding. I grab it and struggle to pull all forty-seven inches of myself up. I try the window. It's unlocked. With a few failed pushes, I make progress on the fourth shove. My small fingers don't help the situation. The window is open.

Swinging one stubby leg over into the bedroom and dragging the other one behind me, I let my body freefall to the floor.

I lose one of my prized Roo sneakers. Lavender and velvet soft to the touch, but Mama says my sneakers are too flamboyant for a boy. Says Sister shouldn't have let me pick them out. I don't know what flamboyant means, but saying the word out loud and watching Mama's brow crinkle makes my skin tingle.

I pick myself up off the worn oak floor and notice the single twin bed. A butter-yellow chenille spread invites me. I take a seat. The bed is neat. My knee peeks through the hole in my faded jeans. I smooth the loose threads just like I've seen Sister do with her smart shirt dresses. Maybe Sister will take me to buy some new jeans. Jeans without holes.

My eyes scan old neighbor lady's room. I settle on a dressing table. A lady's dressing table. All curves. I breathe in the sweet smell of almonds. The smell of sophistication. I push myself off the bed and toward the dressing table. A piece of furniture like this says a lot about a person.

I run my hands over the top of it and notice the chipped polish on my fingernails. Sister left the polish in the bathroom, and I helped myself when no one was looking.

My eyes settle on a gold tube of lipstick: *Cherries in the Snow*. Such a beautiful name and yet so ridiculous. "Cherries in the snow," I say to the empty room. That's not even a real thing.

I reach for it and instantly feel glamorous. Mama's magazines have ads for Cherries in the Snow.

"Does any man really understand you?"

"Makes your lips look good enough to eat! He'll think so, too."

Mama says red lipstick is garish. It's for trollops. Guess old neighbor lady was a trollop. I want to be a trollop too.

I rummage through the drawers. No mustache comb. No musky cologne. No trace of anyone but old neighbor lady. Her white-gold Omega cocktail watch rests in a small velvet-lined tray. I model it on my wrist even though the clasp is broken.

I place the watch back in its velvet bed and knock the lipstick over, catching it before it rolls off. Pulling the gold top off the tube gives me another urge, another tingle. I lean in toward the mirror and part my lips in preparation for my transformation. Cherries in the Snow saturates my lips. I admire my bright mouth, and I smile.

Tilly Troublefield Is Up to No Good

A heady mix of sugar and butter was trapped in Tilly's kitchen, so overwhelming that she almost felt high. The baking itself wasn't her drug. Winning was. And that's what she intended to do at the Piedmont Interstate Fair.

The Piedmont Interstate Fair didn't look like much to an outsider. It was a half-mile dirt track. But what those outsiders didn't know was that track represented a long line of winners. It used to hold the NASCAR Grand National races in the fifties and sixties. Winners had taken victory laps on that very track, and Tilly would be no different.

Each October, the leaves started to turn and a nip edged its way into the air. The change in seasons brought back memories for Tilly. As a kid, she was most interested in standing under the Zipper carnival ride and collecting the change that fell out of the riders' pockets. She can still smell the freshly fried donuts and the apple cider.

She can also still feel the sting of being ignored. She was an average kid with average looks and average abilities. And she was forgotten. It was as if Tilly didn't exist to her peers or their parents. In a sea of classmates with a list of superlatives after their names in the yearbook, there was B-average Tilly.

Of course, the past didn't matter now. Tilly was the reigning queen of the Best in Baked Goods category and Best Overall category in the Piedmont Interstate Fair. Her lemon pound cake, complete with fresh lemon zest glaze, had earned her a decade of accolades. So many, in fact, that she had been featured in a national newspaper.

Boy, those classmates paid attention now. They were shoving orders and cash at Tilly faster than she could make the pound cakes. She had been part of every family birthday party in town, and business was not slowing down. But today there were no birthdays on the schedule. Today was all about Tilly and all about winning. She was on her way to the fairgrounds to admire her blue ribbons.

Tilly made her way to the agricultural building. It was well over 100 years old and the perfect backdrop to display the culinary talent in the community. As she made her way in, friendly hands patted her on the back and greeted her with admiring smiles. Tilly felt electric. She was beaming.

As she made her way into the prize room and toward the long table draped in a pristine white cloth, her eyes went right to her lemon pound cake. Something was wrong: There was only one small blue ribbon draped across her cake. Where was her Best Overall ribbon? Her eyes frantically searched the table and finally rested on a mason jar full of whole figs and cinnamon sticks. There was her grand prize ribbon.

Tilly struggled for air as if the oxygen was being sucked right out of the prize room. The chatter intensified around her. She could feel the judgment and the smugness roll off the others and push up against her. Who had stolen her grand prize?

She went straight to that fig jar. The card said they were

pickled figs. Pickled figs? Who had ever heard of such nonsense? A neighbor came up beside her.

"Pickled figs. Can you believe it, Tilly? I had a small taste when Mr. Ross was experimenting. Taste just like a bread and butter pickle with a little kick. Pure genius, I tell you."

Tilly nodded and offered the neighbor a tight smile. She moved along. Mr. Ross was fairly new to the area, a widow from a few towns over who had wanted a fresh start. And now his fresh start had spilled over into Tilly's life. She was fuming.

As Tilly exited the agricultural building, she spotted the fair director near the funnel cake cart. She cast her eyes down to avoid conversation. It didn't work.

"Tilly! Tilly! Congratulations on your baked goods win. I can't wait to get a sample of that lemon pound cake at tomorrow's celebration of winners."

Tilly politely nodded and kept moving. As she exited the fairgrounds gate, she felt her nails ripping into her palms. Opening her hands, she saw that she had drawn blood. Her own blood. What was Mr. Ross up to? How had a jar of pickled gonad lookalikes beat out her perfect balance of sweet and sour lemon pound cake? In a flash, Tilly knew what she would do. This would not stand.

It was tradition that each winner brings enough of the prize-winning treat to the celebration of winners' ceremony. The judges and the winners would visit and sample the prized goods, while the press would snap photos and interview the attendees. If new experiences were what they wanted, then Tilly was going to give it to them.

As Tilly prepared the batter for her lemon pound cake, she peered out the window over the sink. Her potted plant arrangement was gorgeous—all fall mums, marigolds, and chrysanthemums. Nestled between all the oranges, reds, and golds was a plant with shiny dark berries: her belladonna plant that she had grown from seed herself. Tilly knew the juice from those almost-black berries would blend right in with her lemon glaze for the pound cake.

Days later and countless hours spent in the kitchen, and Tilly was ready for the celebration of winners' event. Judges, contestants, friends and family, and the press gathered in the agricultural building to sample the prize-capturing treats. As the 4-H youth members ferried her cakes from the car to the building, Tilly supervised, pressing her lips together so tight they went numb.

The table groaned under the weight; it looked like the Lord's Supper but the Southern edition. Everyone's plate was weighed down with slivers of cakes, dabs of preserves, and those damn pickled figs. Tilly spied her lemon pound cake with its special glaze on most everyone's plate. A panic ran through her like a sprinkler system, soaking her in sweat. What if a sliver of lemon pound cake wasn't enough?

The room was full of people, chatter, and egos. Tilly stayed in a corner with her plate and one of those pickled figs staring back at her like a wet slug. How could something so ugly be the overall winner? She inhaled deeply and plucked the whole fig from the plate, dropping it into her mouth. Her mouth was filled with a mix of vinegar, sugar, and spices in a perfect layer. Exquisite.

One week after the celebration of winners' event, and Tilly had three fewer neighbors. Most had recovered from the poisoning, but not the unlucky handful that indulged in more than their fair share. Of course, the majority were still battling some aftereffects that lingered.

Tilly pulled two persimmon Fiestaware cake plates from her upper cabinet and two silver forks with the initials *TT* on each handle. She cut two large slices of her prize-winning lemon pound cake complete with special glaze. The doorbell rang. Mr. Ross had arrived.

"Tilly. You look lovely this afternoon. So nice of you to invite me over."

She led Mr. Ross to the cheery yellow kitchen and seated him in front of the largest slice of cake. Next year, the Best Overall category would be with its rightful owner again.

The Interstate Cowboy

The house is bustling with looky-loos dressed in black. Like a bunch of terribly uncool Johnny Cash impersonators. The bench empty next to me. He's not here to smirk at my joke and share a Lucky Strike.

He was my longest relationship. Likely because he spent over half of the year on the road, usually driving up and down the interstate pulling things other people bought. My interstate cowboy. He never overpowered a bucking bull. He tamed America's interstates.

As my feet dangle inches from the ground, the hum of mourners fades, and his voice pierces the screened bedroom window. I close my eyes to soak in the memory.

"Baby, get on in here or I'm gonna start without you."

He flips through the prized record collection, hooking his thumb between Conway Twitty and The Oak Ridge Boys. An easy choice. He continues the search, stopping again between Ronnie Milsap and George Strait. He doesn't believe in alphabetizing. Instead, he organizes by his tastes.

The opening notes of a lonely violin float from the bedroom window to my ears, and a slow smile starts on his face. The first few words of "Amarillo By Morning" land on him, and the tension in his shoulders releases. It is a George Strait day.

As George begins singing about his life that stole a girlfriend and a wife, I stretch my legs on the bench, immersed in my memory as if it is happening now. I inhale the un-filtered tobacco, biting at my throat. He wraps his arms around me and scoots us around the room, hand pressed in on my lower back.

George's crooning fades. My eyes flutter open, body pushing to stay put on the bench rather than venturing inside amongst the grieving and greedy. Doubt his kids will let me stay here seeing as how my name isn't on the house, and we weren't even common law. They've already laid claim to the rig.

We had big plans. He was on a fast path to retirement, and then we were going to see the world. A stop at Paul Bunyan's Fry Pan in Montana. A swirl cone at Little America Travel Center in Wyoming. Of course, the Cadillac Ranch was at the tip-top of our list. Then perhaps a stop in Two Guns, Arizona.

I grind my cigarette out on the bench and slam my feet on the ground.

The Seasons of Gilly Black

Mole Ramsey scampered under the fence that divided the "haves" from the "have nots." He didn't know what either of those meant, but he heard his mama say it all the time. His sister Gloria's voice carried over the fence. The smack of the tennis ball on the racket made his teeth hurt. Gloria would invite the neighbor boys over in the summer to play tennis, and Mole usually took the opportunity to avoid the drama.

At twelve, he was just shy of being two years younger than Gloria. Mole wasn't his real name, but it was the only thing anyone called him. Gilliard Black, or Gilly to most that knew him, gave him the nickname on account of how he could scurry under the fence that divided his parents' estate from Gilly's farm. When Gloria and her boyfriends took over the house, he would scurry under the fence to spy on Gilly.

Mole heard his mama talk about Gilly and how he hadn't been the same since coming back from the war. Looked like she wanted to spit talking about their neighbor. No compassion. And his mama would never spit. His mama couldn't understand how the school let Gilly drive that bus full of kids. But the highlight of Mole's morning and afternoon consisted of Gilly tipping his Red Man Chew hat at him when those bus doors opened.

School was hard for Mole. His family was too well off

for most of the cliques, but Mole was not refined enough for the one that was his birthright. He wanted to belong. Wanted someone to look forward to seeing him when he got off that bus in the afternoons. Instead, all Mole got was the turned backs of his classmates. But Gilly's place was home to him.

Mole liked to be close to Gilly. Once in a while, he would make himself known, and Gilly would chat with him. His favorite thing was to stroll through Gilly's expansive garden and then take an afternoon nap amongst the tomato plants. He never saw any tomatoes on those plants, but it's what Gilly said they were.

Mole ran his hands through the large spiky leaves. The greens varied from light to dark. Smelled like a skunk had sprayed them, and yet the smell was oddly pleasing to him. His absolute favorite part of sneaking over to Gilly's was sitting on the top step of the porch while Gilly and his old war buddies visited.

There wasn't laughter, but there was an easiness between them. Mole sensed they understood each other, and in turn understood him. They too knew what it was like to be cast aside and ignored. They had a ritual, and Mole was infatuated with it.

At each afternoon visit, Mole would watch as Gilly pulled a small sack out of his back pocket and laid it on a table alongside his rolling papers. Mole paid special attention to how gentle Gilly was with the whole process, delicately licking the rolling paper at the end to give it just enough moisture to secure it. Then he would pass that cigarette around his group of buddies, always sharing. Gilly was a giver. It's what Mole liked about him most.

One day, a buddy of Gilly's passed that cigarette to Mole. He froze, unsure of what to do next but desperate to belong. Gilly shook his head no and said, "Mole don't need that. He's fine with our company."

On those afternoons, Mole would stretch out full length on the top step of the porch. He'd close his eyes and enjoy the earthy scent from the cigarette being passed around. Why they shared one cigarette he didn't know, but he wasn't going to risk asking questions and not be invited back.

He'd overheard their conversations.

I'll pay you for it, Gilly.

No. You know I don't charge.

It ain't right of me to not give you something back.

You give me your friendship. It's enough.

These words would float around Mole and mingle with the smoke, pulling him into a peaceful dreamlike state.

On his way back to his side of the fence, he'd run his hands over those tomato leaves, willing them to release their stench.

The lush summer grass was replaced with a blanket of leaves in vibrant reds and yellows. Mole still wrestled his body under Gilly's fence. Didn't matter the season. One day after a particularly long afternoon at Gilly's, he slid through the back door as not to disturb his mama. He didn't see her standing by the kitchen sink. His mama's eyes drew together making a deep eleven between her eyebrows. She was scared.

"You reek of trash. I've told you not to go over there."

She kept her eyes on the window, squinting as if she were trying to see all the way to Gilly's. Mole stood at the back door attempting to fold himself into something so small his mama wouldn't notice him. His mama's body softened as she turned to him.

"I wish I knew what drew you under that fence. I wish I knew, so I could undo it."

Mole stayed by the door. Not moving in case his mama forgot he was there and let him be invisible again.

"Go on and get washed up. We're going to eat soon. You can help your sister set the table."

Mole bolted from the door to his room. He didn't understand what Mama and the others in town had against Gilly. Why were they scared of him? All he had seen of Gilly was how he cared for others. What Mama saw as a darkness Mole saw as a sadness. A blanket that lay over Gilly's heart trying to smother happiness like it was a fire.

Fall had turned to winter, and the red dirt was packed down hard from the cold. The frozen dirt crumbled under Mole's knees as he scurried under Gilly's fence. He'd seen the smoke rising high in the sky like a signal to him. Gilly was burning trash, which meant he was standing somewhere close by. Mole didn't want to miss his chance to be next to Gilly. See if he could uncover that sadness that seemed to follow his neighbor around.

He found Gilly right close to the fire. He was holding some photos and some letters. Mole didn't ask to see the photos out of fear he'd be sent away. He tucked himself in tight in the hopes that Gilly wouldn't even realize he was there. It was enough for Mole to just be close.

He watched Gilly looking at the black-and-white photographs, craning his neck for a peep himself. Mole spied a woman in the photograph. Gilly was in it too. He had his arm slung over the woman's shoulders, making her look like a child's dolly rather than a woman. Her hair was so black and shiny, like an oil slick. He realized the photograph was shaking. Gilly was shaking, but no noise was coming out.

It was as if Gilly's body couldn't contain his emotions anymore, and Mole watched as the shaking escaped Gilly in sobs. His neighbor's knees fell to the ground and the photographs fluttered close to the fire. Mole snatched them up and pressed them to his chest face down so as not to intrude on Gilly's pain. Seemed like the right thing to do. Mole waited patiently while Gilly sobbed, allowing his neighbor, his friend, to let all that pent-up sadness release. But Mole had a hunch it would just fill an empty space inside of Gilly again, pushing and shoving itself further and further into his body until it was all dark.

Gilly got to his feet and pulled a yellowed handkerchief from his back pocket and mopped his face. Mole continued to clutch the photographs to his chest.

"Mole, you ever just have something push at you? Push at your insides until it just spills right out 'cause it ain't got nowhere else to go?"

Mole nodded. He knew exactly how that felt. His sister Gloria pushed him out. His mama pushed him out. Most of the kids at school didn't mean to push him out, but they just weren't interested in what Mole was interested in. They made him feel like he had twenty years on them rather than the preteen boy that he was.

"I just left her there. I left them all there. We were supposed to be there to help those people. But that ain't what we did there."

Mole nodded again. He wanted to comfort his friend, but he sensed that Gilly had more to say. More he must say.

"I can't close my eyes without being back over there. Thought maybe if I burned those then it would disappear. That I could forget I ever went. But the mind don't work like that, Mole. Just don't work like that."

Mole made eye contact with Gilly, and then he laid his hand on Gilly's back, patting at it awkwardly like he'd seen the men do when they were on the porch smoking.

"Thank you, Mole. You're a good boy. A good person. Your mama must be real proud of you."

Without thinking first, Mole piped up, "She's not. She don't even know who I am."

It was Gilly's turn to awkwardly pat Mole on the back.

"The people we love. The people that love us back, well, they can have the hardest time seeing who we are. I bet your mama is proud of you. She just don't have the right words to say it."

Mole wasn't convinced, but he followed Gilly up to the porch and watched him pull his baggie and rolling papers out. His ritual. Mole stretched out on the top step and let the sun warm his body as the skunky smoke wafted over his face.

Winter stretched to summer, and Mole's routine of slipping under the fence continued. He passed his days with Gilly and his buddies, stretched out on the top step baking himself brown like a cake of cornbread. Soon August turned to September, and another school year found Mole. He hated to see the summer leave. He'd enjoyed his time spent in Gilly's garden and on his porch. He hadn't even minded the smack of the tennis balls courtesy of Gloria and her parade of boys.

It was the first week of school when Gilly got fired. Mole had been on the school bus the day Gilly lost it. At least that's what the townsfolk called the incident: "losing it." But if Jimmy Hambright and Doyle McClain hadn't been teasing Artie Hunnwacker for being a girl that dips snuff, then there wouldn't have been no incident for the town folk to yammer about. Gilly had grabbed those boys by their scruffs, dragged them off his bus, and whacked them both right in the kissers. When Jimmy and Doyle climbed back up those steps, they didn't even turn their bodies Artie's way. But Mole was alone in thinking that Gilly was a champion of the underdog.

The bus ride to school used to be Mole's favorite part because Gilly was behind the wheel. Mole missed his friend, but he still scurried under the fence as soon as his feet left the bus each day.

Mole's ritual began one afternoon: feet slapping down on the asphalt and carrying him to the fence. He rolled under and stopped at the tomato plants, running his hands through them so they'd release their stench. He caught a whiff of smoke in the air. He could hear his mama calling his name, but he chose to let her voice drift away and let his body pull him toward the smoke.

As he made his way out of the row of tomato plants, he saw the bottoms of Gilly's shoes. Puzzled, he stopped. He could still hear his mama calling his name, but he continued to ignore her. Sounded like her voice was closer though.

Mole's mind was telling him to stay put, but his feet moved him forward. He peeped around the edge of the tomato plants and saw Gilly. He was on his back next to the smoldering fire. The black-and-white photographs Mole had seen were scattered around him. He ran to his friend. There was a neat hole in the side of Gilly's head and a small revolver at his side; a photograph fluttered into what was left of the fire. Mole scooted over on his knees and pulled it out of the ashes just as the woman with the oil-slick black hair's face started to curl up from the heat.

Gilly's service was simple and quick. The same men that had flooded his porch with stories and smoke showed up to bid him farewell. As they folded the American flag draped over Gilly's coffin, Mole watched to see who they would give it to. A man laid it beside a charred and wrinkled framed photo of the woman with oil-slick black hair. Tears dripped down Mole's face and soaked into his shirt front. One of Gilly's friends put his hand on Mole's shoulder.

"Drop by the porch. The fellas are going to gather this afternoon."

Mole nodded. His mama had brought him to the funeral, but she wouldn't get out of the car. Stayed inside the giant

Cadillac working on her cross stitch. But he knew he would slip away and scoot under the fence.

Later that day, Mole lay across the top step of Gilly's porch. He didn't understand exactly what had unfolded, but he knew he was different now. No longer a boy. He listened as the friends' words and smoke swirled above his head and blanketed him in comfort. Gilly Black had seen Mole's own sadness inside of him. Been the only person to acknowledge it. Tell him it would be ok, and there was light on the other side. Mole had seen through Gilly's sadness too.

As Mole's eyes closed and he drifted off to the sound of Gilly's friends weaving tales about their friend, he felt a slight nip to the air. Fall was coming.

All Women Marry Down and Other Fatherly Advice

June stared into the casket. Daddy was gray like a clouded day. The mortician had sworn up and down that he would look like himself. That's exactly what he had said. "Your father will look like himself. Just like he's fallen asleep peacefully."

Must be how they upsell you. Make you think you can still connect with your loved one somehow.

June could still hear her daddy's accent when she thought of the advice he would give—the advice that rolled off the man's tongue like a silk scarf against your skin. Soft and subtle but leaving you with the feeling of its presence long after it was gone.

And now here she was with no one else left. No one who looked like her. No one who sounded like her.

June's daddy was all she ever had. He was all she ever needed.

The mortician's eyes bore down on the back of her neck. Curious. Maybe some judgment. She didn't give one good goddamn. This thought made her smile. More advice from Daddy.

He would say, "June bug, don't you give one good goddamn what other people think you should do. You do what you feel is right."

Of course, Daddy's advice wasn't always so clear. He also

loved to tell her, "All you need in life is slim hips and influential friends." Then he would slap his knee and double over in laughter at his own self. Daddy thought he was right funny. He had his moments.

When June turned eighteen, Daddy had some advice about relationships.

He'd say, "June bug, all women marry down. Even your mama did."

This stuck with June. Daddy never talked about Mama. And he didn't double over in laughter at this one.

He would stare at her hard. Almost as if he was making sure this piece of advice stuck. She often wondered if Daddy was warning her not to settle for a man like himself.

At twenty, June brought home Joe Boy. Daddy had not been pleased—so June married him. Of all the times to not listen to Daddy's advice.

Now June stood over Daddy all by herself. No Joe Boy. He'd fled not long after the marriage ceremony. Turned out Daddy had been right.

So here June was. All by her lonesome. As she leaned over to tell Daddy goodbye she whispered, "Don't worry, Daddy. Mama didn't marry down."

Self-Care with Cher

The cold nips at my nose, turning it on like a drippy spigot. Damn dog's digestive system pushes me off the warm couch each winter evening right before 9:00 p.m. The darkness makes the temperature feel even more bitter as I stand on my front lawn, nose dripping and tiny terrier nipping at the leaves as they drift to the ground.

I secure my fanny pack. Flashlight? Check. Poop bags? Check. Pepper spray? Check. All secured in my middle-aged sack of sensibility. My nine-pound dog strains at the end of her leash like a bucking bull being held back in a steel pen. It's Friday night. I'm forty-five years old. And this is my life.

I pull my toboggan down over my numb ears. The dog is charging forward unaffected by the cold. As we set off, four cars pass us like they're in a fast funeral procession. I navigate the eager terrier to someone's yard and hope I don't step in some self-centered neighbor's dog shit that wasn't picked up.

We round the corner, navigating from the busy section of the neighborhood to the less traveled and settle in at a good clip. Tomorrow is trash day, which means the dog has a buffet of cardboard and discards to stop and pee on. Everyone must know that the neighborhood trash belongs to her. Each time we stop at a trash pile, a throbbing heat sets in my center and radiates out toward my arms and legs. How something can be throbbing and numb at the same time is beyond me, yet here I am.

I kick at a box and say, "Don't mess with that. There could be a severed head in it." The dog looks at me with such pity. I shrug. Both of us perk up at a sound that is out of place. Clink. We hear it again. Could it be? Yes, that is the sound of a bottle, a small one, hitting the pavement. Next, a sweet voice travels from further up the road through the frozen pavement and toward my toes up to my chest. I start to thaw a bit. The voice has reached to the tips of the tiny terrier's oversized ears, and her short legs are tap, tap, tapping away.

We've reached the part of our walk—the part of our night— hell, the part of our very day that we look forward to. The part that makes all the preparations worth it. The joyous lady who sings Cher is coming. She is on her way, and she is bringing us a nip to warm and revive our tired bones.

I hear her approach before I see her car. It's like Cher is in my neighborhood, and she is begging me to answer her question. Yes, Cher, I do believe in life after love. I do. I too told my mom I am a rich man and don't need to marry one. So not true, but I get caught up in moments.

A Nissan Pathfinder rounds the bend in the road and heads toward me and the dog. We're both energized now. Clink. Another tiny bottle flies out of the Nissan's window. The smell of warm cinnamon nips at my nose. God, I love this moment each night. A moment that is just mine. No one else around except my best friend and Cher.

She slows a bit as she approaches us. We make eye contact. Her slim arm hangs out of the car window revealing a large tattoo of Ruth Bader Ginsberg. She shakes a mini bottle of

Fireball at me and raises an eyebrow like the musical booze fairy she is. I snatch it, crack the seal, and take a quick swig. The sweetness mixes perfectly with the hot cinnamon as it burns through my throat and settles in my belly. Cher is now belting out about turning back time, and while I love the music, I am not interested in turning back time. I want to savor this moment. Savor the hot cinnamon. Savor the cold. The freedom.

She pulls away from us with a short squeal from her tires. It's just me and the tiny terrier now. I pull the zipper of my jacket up higher and cover my mouth. We head toward home to thaw.

6:00 a.m. comes early: another day on the hamster wheel that is my life. Take care of the dog. Take care of the house. Go to work and take care of those people. All of that just to turn around and take care of the dog again.

We bundle up, and the tiny terrier is not pulling at the leash this morning. She is content to stay in the warm bed. I drag her down the road, and she sniffs at those same cardboard boxes but looks at me as if to say, "Where is the magic this morning?" And she's right. Something is missing.

We turn the same corner to take us from the busy part of the neighborhood to the less traveled. The dog stops to relieve herself. Our hearts just aren't in this. I turn us around to head home, and my foot kicks something. Clink. A familiar sound. I look down and pick up a mini bottle of Fireball. The seal is still intact.

I snatch it up and put the magic in my pocket. Lord knows I'll need it later.

Acknowledgments

Many thanks to the journals where these pieces first appeared:

"My Diesel Ghost," *Flash Fiction Magazine*

"Origami," *Months to Years*

"Lessons Learned," *The Citron Review*

"Francine Pascal Goes to Bible Camp," *Call Me [Out]*

"Becoming Linda," *JAKE*

"That Time Strom Thurmond Almost Ruined My Family Day," *Salvation South*

"Restless," *Pigeon Review*

"A Night Out with Big Ricky," *Cowboy Jamboree*

"The Ballad of Sugar and Doo," *Salvation South*

"A Glamorous Life," *Reckon Review*

"In the Garden," *The Dead Mule School of Southern Literature*

"Paper Dolls," *Montana Mouthful*, reprinted in *SugarSugarSalt Magazine*

"Black Walnuts," *Door is a Jar*

"All That Glitters," *Final Girl Bulletin Board*

"I Am Shitty Bitty," *Potato Soup Journal*

"The Invisible Woman," *Bright Flash Literary Review*

"Grief's Watermark," *Coalesce Community*, reprinted in *Bulb Culture Collective*

"Welcome to the Starlite," *Idle Ink*

"Cherries in the Snow," *Gastropoda*
"Tilly Troublefield Is Up to No Good," *Roi Faineant*
"The Interstate Cowboy," *The Airgonaut*
"The Seasons of Gilly Black," *BULL*
"All Women Marry Down and Other Fatherly Advice," *The Dead Mule School of Southern Literature*
"Self-Care with Cher," *Corvus Review*

These stories are deeply rooted in my family and the places I spent time exploring as a kid. Each one was born from conversations with my daddy around the dinner table. Without him, there would be no starting place.

To the writers who blurbed this collection: Amy Cipolla Barnes, Meagan Lucas, and Adam Van Winkle. I admired your work and couldn't believe it when you all thought mine was worthy. Go buy their books.

To my writing group: Andrew, Gillian, Jerry, and Kathleen. Y'all are my bright spot while trudging through the writing trenches.

To the journals that took a chance on me and made me feel like maybe I could do this.

To Charlotte Hamrick for being a cheerleader for my work. Having you take the time to read my stories and share them was a constant boost for me.

To Damon McKinney for letting me pepper him with a thousand writing and publishing questions and always being so gracious.

To Sheldon Compton for leaving his inbox open to me and always responding.

To Jen Hawkins for pushing me to even begin this journey.

To my publisher and editor, Casie Dodd, who is one of the kindest people out there in the literary world. You are the only one I considered for this collection, and I'm forever grateful it has a home with you.

To the three teachers who told me to keep writing: Barbara Latham, Jennifer Heinsohn, and Chris White.

To my friends: Amanda for never being afraid of my first drafts. Heather Kay for constantly reminding me that I am in fact a writer. My Simpsonville girls for making me leave the house when I was way down in it. To my work besties, Brittany and Sierra, for always checking in and asking what I'm working on. To all of my Avett music ladies that kept the group chat open no matter how late it was. I love you all.

To my Sissy, my mom, my dad, JHT, and Josh, who never flinch when I jot something they've said or done down in my trusty notebook.

To my oldest sister, Kelley. I miss you in ways I didn't know existed. I feel you cheering me on.

And to Alex. Always.

KATY GOFORTH is a writer and editor for a national engineering and surveying organization in Greenville, South Carolina. Her writing has appeared in *Brevity*, *Reckon Review*, *Cowboy Jamboree*, *Salvation South*, and other journals. She has been nominated for *Best American Short Stories* and *Best Small Fictions*. *Anchored* is her first book. Her novel *Traveling Alone* is forthcoming. She was born and raised in South Carolina and lives with her spouse and two pups, Finn and Betty Anne. Learn more at katygoforth.com.

Belle Point Press is a literary small press along the Arkansas-Oklahoma border. Our mission is simple: Stick around and read. Learn more at bellepointpress.com.

BELLE
POINT
PRESS